The HOME SHARE

♥

SALLY CLEMENTS

For my friend, Maya.
Without whom, this book would never have been written.

ISBN Print Edition: 9798857597422

Cover Art: https://yummybookcovers.com/

Editing: https://edmcreatingperfection.wordpress.com/

Note for readers: I normally have my books edited with an American English edit, but this time it suited the story to use a UK/hiberno English edit. As such, you may notice regional differences!

Chapter One

We have seven days.

Evie Andrews forced down the feeling of panic and walked faster.

"Stop wriggling." She tightened her grip and pressed the doorbell with her other hand. She'd slept fitfully last night and, as a result, had dozed through her alarm. She peered through the stained-glass panels next to the front door, just making out a shadowy figure shuffling towards them.

"Good morning, Your Majesty." The old lady focused all her attention on the cat in Evie's arms. "Come on in."

Evie put Cleo down. The cat dashed in and made straight for the kitchen.

"Morning, Eleanore." Evie smiled at her neighbour. She handed over a plastic bag full of silver sachets of cat food. "Here are today's food choices. Her Majesty is liking duck this week, but I put a couple of chicken sachets in there too, just in case. You know how she changes her mind."

Eleanore took the bag and nodded. "Any news on the house hunt?"

Sale boards decorated the front gardens of half the houses on the leafy Dublin street, including the one she and her flatmate Soo had called home for the past year. Stratospheric house prices made selling the more attractive option. As a result, rental properties were few and far between. Soo moved in with her boyfriend, but Evie and Cleopatra were still looking. And running out of time.

"Nothing yet." She glanced over to the house next door where she and Cleopatra lived. "They have back-to-back viewings today."

"Don't worry, Cleo will be safe here."

Eleanore didn't ask if Evie wanted to come in for a coffee. That wasn't part of their routine. Their routine was simple. Evie delivered her cat across the short distance between their two houses every morning, and she picked her up after work every evening. The arrangement suited them both. Eleanore was usually busy in the evenings but enjoyed the cat's company during the day.

When they'd moved into the flat in Bedford Street a year ago, Cleo had ventured out daily from the cat flap on adventures unknown until Evie spotted her coming out of the house next door. She'd been worried that her cat was sick; she'd stopped eating but didn't seem to have lost weight. But a quick chat with the elderly lady next door revealed the cat's secret. Cleo shared the love by spending her time equally between them. And who could blame her? A warm fire and food and drink on tap beat spending the day home alone.

Evie was happy to share. Especially now that she needed someone to mind Cleo while troupes of mucky strangers tracked across her carpet and poked around in her cupboards daily. She hated the thought of her space being invaded while she was at work, but what could she do? The estate agent was apologetic but firm. She would stay with potential buyers all the time they were in the house, but as a renter with days left on her lease, Evie had no rights.

Finding another flat in Dublin was difficult. And finding somewhere to rent that allowed pets proving to be impossible. But living without Cleopatra wasn't an option. The cat had already suffered a big upset in her life with the death of her previous owner, which saw them move from the country's relative safety to a big city.

She'd handled it well, and in the past year, she'd settled into a familiar routine. Evie didn't know how Cleo would cope in yet another strange place.

Evie's mother had loved the cat unconditionally, just the way Evie now did. Keeping the little feline alive and well was Evie's main objective in life. Cleopatra was family. She couldn't let her family down.

"I better head. I'll be late."

Eleanore stepped back. "See you later."

Evie spent her day driving but took public transport to work. This morning a bus broke down while pulling out into traffic, blocking two lanes, and causing traffic to back up for half a mile. When she reached the bright yellow DUKW parked up at the embarkation spot on St Stephen's Green, Oscar was waiting for the passengers to arrive.

She picked up the pace. "Sorry, the traffic was terrible."

Oscar was a big man. At her and Soo's fancy dress party last Halloween, he and his wife had come as Fred and Wilma Flintstone. If there had been a prize, they would have won it. His thick dark hair was overlong, and his bushy beard needed taming.

Or rather, it would need taming if it were not an essential part of his rough Viking look. He wore a plain, unbleached cotton tunic topped with a sheepskin cloak adapted from something bought at IKEA. Necklaces of shells and runes tied to leather strips hung around his neck. No jeans for Oscar. The bottom half of his body was clad in homemade rough trousers and primitive leather sandals.

Drunks who met him on his way home after a shift blinked and thought they'd seen a hairy Viking ghost.

Oscar scratched the back of his head. "No problem. I drove

past your house last night and saw they've planted a sign." His face twisted into his sympathetic impression. "No chance they'll take it off the market, then?"

"None. Cleo and I are still looking for somewhere, but there's not much out there."

"Pets is the problem, isn't it?" Oscar gripped her shoulder with a meaty hand. "If people could see how much you love that cat, they'd know you wouldn't go anywhere without her. She's family."

A group of people in their twenties approached. They huddled together, taking selfies before the chunky yellow vehicle, smiling and laughing. Obviously not related. But closer than close.

"This lot looks ready for fun."

Oscar's wide grin flashed white. "They do. They might not share blood, but you don't need to be born to the same parents to be family."

His gaze shifted as they got ready to board. "Yes. This is where you start the tour." He flicked down the metal steps and pulled up the scanner on his cell phone. "Tickets?"

Evie climbed aboard and checked the dash. Driving a World War Two amphibious vehicle around Dublin with a crew of tourists wearing plastic Viking helmets wasn't what she'd envisioned after her history degree from Trinity, but she wouldn't change it for the sad sterility of a life inside behind a desk.

On the streets of Dublin with Oscar or one of the other guides beside her, she could appreciate all the city had to offer. And had always had to offer through the centuries. Driving through the backstreets, illuminating places shrouded in the shadows of time and shining a light that pierced those shadows to reveal the city as it was in a previous era, was exciting.

As she drove down a narrow alley off St Stephen's Green, she could almost see the body snatchers dragging bodies ripped from freshly dug graves and stuffing them into sacks to sell to medical students at the College of Surgeons.

And every time she manoeuvred the big vehicle around Christchurch while the guide spoke of the Viking settlement beneath her wheels, part of her appreciated the wind on her face, as ancient Norse had done in the same spot. People separated by time, but not place. The layers of hidden humanity. Ghosts that walk amongst us. Taking the time to see the city through the eyes of the tourists brought it into focus. The buildings with carved granite words above their mantels revealing their original purpose. The beautiful faience panels on the front of the Italianate Sunlight Chambers building at the corner of Parliament Street. How many people take the time to look up and notice this late nineteenth-century frieze depicting the history of hygiene?

History was everywhere. All around. Doing this job meant she could enjoy the city every day. Maybe one day, driving the funny yellow vehicle would cease to spark excitement, but right now, it filled her soul.

"Okay, this fella here. Let's give him a roar." Oscar waved to his side as his words rang out over the onboard PA system.

Every tour followed a familiar pattern. The passengers boarded and donned plastic Viking helmets with horns, then proceeded around the city roaring like marauding Vikings at passers-by. Native pedestrians took being roared at by a tin full of tourists in their stride as they walked around. Some started roaring first in a pre-emptive strike, knowing they'd be rewarded by an echoing roar from the Duck.

Others were coy. They braced their shoulders and stared at the pavement with self-conscious half smiles as they heard themselves singled out for attention. They inevitably grinned when the shout rang out.

The people in the Duck were having fun. Pure, unadulterated fun. The sort of fun little kids had, jumping out of cupboards onto their parents after hide and seek. Every encounter made Evie smile.

But this one was different.

The man sauntering in the Dublin sunshine had earbuds in. Even for the morning commute, he was sharply dressed in a charcoal-grey suit and a pale-blue shirt. His midnight-black hair showed a hint of a wave and rested a couple of inches below his collar.

He walked to a different beat. To the rhythm of the music flowing into his ears. He strode in front of them. Oblivious to the impending roar. Evie glanced at Oscar. She wanted this one to escape. Knew, with some weird, unfamiliar instinct, that this wouldn't go well. She opened her mouth to warn Oscar, but it was too late.

"One, Two—"

The victim lifted his takeout coffee cup to his lips.

"Three."

A deafening roar rang out. There wasn't a person alive who couldn't hear it.

Mystery man jumped. The coffee splashed onto the ground, wetting the front of his shirt and trousers as it did. He spun around, arms wide. Eyes full of fury. Directed at the passengers. Whose demeanour had changed. Instead of laughing, they looked chastened and embarrassed. Aware that they'd inadvertently messed up a stranger's day.

"I'm sorry, mate! Telephone the office, and we'll buy you another shirt." Oscar gestured to the side of the vehicle. "The number's on the side."

The stranger planted his hands on his hips. Glowered.

Then his gaze flickered to Evie. She tried to formulate a shaky smile when faced with the blaze of blue under black brows. He glared at her as though it were her fault. Accusingly, as if she should have warned him.

The traffic light was still red, and streams of pedestrians crossed in front of her.

"Sorry," she mouthed.

Then the lights changed. Evie focused on the road. When she risked a look in her side mirror, he remained in the middle of the pavement, with a large wet coffee stain soaking the front of his shirt.

Chapter Two

U n-fucking-believable.

Jake Ridley stared at the departing yellow boat on wheels. He'd dashed out his ear pods on hearing the roar from behind him. Now the offending vehicle trundled off down the road without a care. Leaving a black belch of smoke hanging in the air in its wake.

He assessed his surroundings. He couldn't turn up to his city-centre meeting covered in coffee. He spotted a man's shop and stalked across the road. Ten minutes later, he re-joined the melee clad in a fresh shirt and tie. A considerate shop assistant had found tissues and helped him clean up his suit and shoes. She'd even provided a bag for his soiled shirt and tie. He'd still be early for the meeting if he picked up his pace.

He had to make a good impression. Closing this deal was imperative for his career goals.

He remembered the startled brunette driving the boat/truck thing. She was pretty, in a dark hair, dark eyes, cute haircut way. Somehow incongruous as the driver of such a hefty vehicle. But that impression probably said more about him than it did her. He didn't like to think he suffered from ingrained misogyny, but he doubtless did.

Even without complicated make-up, over-the-top costumes, and an exaggerated hairstyle, the driver had a touch of Princess Amidala about her. She looked shocked at the state of him. The 'sorry' she mouthed seemed heartfelt. And it really wasn't her fault. As they continued down the road, he heard the guide hailing another passer-by, the shout of 'one, two, three,' warning of the following roar.

If Jake hadn't been so engrossed in the soundtrack to *The Greatest Showman*, he would have heard them coming. Wouldn't have thrown his coffee all over himself like an idiot.

He stopped. Checked his phone.

The maps app indicated this was the place. The façade of the building was pale stone, with carved Corinthian columns reaching above the door and topped by a delicate half-circular window, a characteristic Georgian fanlight. A brass plaque fastened to the brick next to the kingfisher-blue front door stated *Sweeney Brothers Ltd*.

This was the place. In minutes Jake was buzzed in, had charmed the receptionist to hold on to his bagged clothing while he was in the meeting, and was ushered into a boardroom.

He was helping himself from the jug of coffee on a side table when a man strolled in. He was blond and looked in his early thirties, with a ruddy complexion and a smile like a happy Labrador.

"Hi, I'm Matt Sweeney." He waved at the hospitality display. "Pastry? The pecan plaits are delicious."

"I had a cinnamon roll for breakfast at the hotel. Coffee will do fine, thanks."

They sat with an expanse of smoky glass between them.

Matt cleared his throat. His foot tapped under the table.

Jake was well used to soothing frazzled nerves. His job made everyone he met in a professional capacity nervous. He forensically investigated companies that were potential acquisition targets for the company he worked for. Global Innovations was a behemoth bringing smaller companies under its corporate umbrella, and this company, Sweeney Brothers, was their latest target. Jake hadn't met either of the brothers before today.

"My brother Cormac isn't able to join us this morning." Matt pushed a hand through his hair. "He has a bad dose of flu. He was determined to attend, but he's so sick..." He shook his head. "We don't want to get it."

"You're right." Time was short. The company had allocated a month to complete the process, which would mean working flat out. He had no time to factor in a few days' sickness.

He pulled a sheaf of papers from his briefcase. He stacked them into three piles and slid one across the table to Matt.

"Today, I'd like to walk you through what's involved in the process."

Matt's shoulders relaxed a fraction.

Jake tapped the middle pile. "This is a full set for Cormac."

"I'll drop it out to him at lunchtime. He's confined to bed, but there's nothing wrong with his brain."

"Fair enough. Page one, then. This is what I'll need from you for the first week."

In the first week of evaluating a potential acquisition, there were a standard number of steps he always took. The first was to meet with the management team to gather information about the business and its operations. They'd be able to cover some of that information today, but he'd need to follow up with Cormac in the next few days.

"I'd like to talk about the company. I've looked at your catalogue of apps, but I want to try to understand what makes them so unique. And I'd like to get a clear picture of how the company operates. What every employee does."

Matt's forehead creased in a micro frown. This too, wasn't unusual. Global Innovations had a reputation for cutting the fat. Honing their acquisitions to their leanest and most efficient. Matt

Sweeney may fear that Global intended to slash his workforce, which might be necessary.

But it was Jake's job to reassure, not heighten Matt's concerns.

"We run a tight ship here. Every employee is needed." Matt crossed his arms. "Making people redundant is a deal breaker."

Jake admired the other man's stance. "Noted. I will look for areas to increase productivity or streamline expenses. My report will go to you for your input and modification, if necessary, before going to Global. I'd like to go through financials tomorrow."

"I have Sean Mulroney, our financial controller, on standby."

"Great." Jake flashed a smile to put Matt at ease. "There's a list on page three of everything I'll need to examine." They flicked through a couple of pages.

"Income statements, balance sheets, cash flow. Fine. I'll pass this on to Sean and make sure he pulls all the paperwork for your meeting."

They spent a few minutes discussing Jake's agenda for the week. After the financials, he wanted to analyse the company's market position and competitive landscape to determine the growth potential. He'd already begun researching trends and macroeconomic factors that could affect the company's future performance.

Jake's cell buzzed on the table, and the screen lit up.

Alison.

He bounced the call. His mother would leave a message. She always did.

Matt said, "We've found you an office."

Jake could work anywhere as long as he had something to sit on and a place to lay out his research. He spent his working life visiting different organisations in different countries and often was confined to a company boardroom, a cramped corner in the canteen, or reduced to dragging suitcases of files into an airless hotel room.

"An office would be fantastic."

"Okay, let's make some headway on this list of yours." Matt rubbed the back of his neck. Rolled his shoulders and waited as Jake flipped to a new clean page of his notebook and uncapped his pen. "Then I'll set you up with your office and introduce you around."

Jake worked solidly until lunch. He ventured outside for coffee and a sandwich, which he brought back. The large corner office had a window with a great panorama over the city. He swivelled the chair around and stared out as he ate.

When he'd finished, he called his mother.

"Finally. I left you a message hours ago." The fact that he worked for a living had escaped Alison Wilde. At least she was consistent. Her number one concern was always her.

"I was in a meeting." Jake sipped his coffee.

"In Ireland. In Dublin." Her tone was accusatory.

"I work all over the world, you know that."

"Yes, but you're in Dublin and didn't let me know. I need you to do..."

A pigeon landed on the windowsill and observed him curiously. It looked hungry.

"Are you listening to me?"

He came back to the present in a rush. "Of course."

"So, what did I say?"

"You need me to do something."

She huffed. And with good reason. He'd zoned out and missed half of the conversation.

"You have a grandmother, you know. Eleanore lives in Dublin. Have you been in contact with her?"

"I plan to." The relationship between his mother and his grandmother was strained at best. Alison was too busy with her life in London to visit, and fundamentally the two women didn't seem to like each other much. Jake hadn't seen her since he was a kid, but he'd always liked her. She was forthright, independent, and genuinely interested in his and his brothers' opinions and ambitions.

But they didn't see much of her. With the benefit of being an adult, the patterns of manipulation were more transparent. Alison wanted to control everything, even her children's relationship with their grandmother. She'd rationed access.

By the time he was old enough to make his own approach, Eleanore was someone he didn't know very well, and living in different countries, there hadn't been an opportunity to meet with her casually and renew those ties.

He didn't even have her telephone number. But he knew where she lived. A short walk from the office he was in now. He'd been counting the hours until he could walk up and knock on her front door. He'd hoped that could be tonight, but the pile of documents before him might mean tomorrow or the day after would be a more realistic target to aim for.

"Your grandmother is eighty-five. My friend Dorothy's mother is eighty-five too, and she fell last week and had to go into a home. Mother is stubborn. She wouldn't tell me if she'd broken both legs. She lives in that huge house on her own. If something happened, she would be alone and left for dead. I don't think it's safe for her to live alone anymore. I rang her last week and told her."

"How did she take that?" Jake made no effort to hide the sarcasm in his voice.

"Well, she wasn't very happy. She told me to mind my own business. That's why it's so useful to have you there, on the spot, as it were. You can visit, evaluate everything, and make recommendations. That's what you do, isn't it? Evaluate?"

Before Jake had a chance to respond, she continued, "You could compile a list of nursing homes and care homes locally. She won't want to move to England. She's always lived in Dublin, and it would seem to be the best place for her."

"I think my grandmother can make her own decisions."

"She's old. She needs help. And there's the whole question of her house. It will need to be put on the market. You could research what other houses near it have reached in the market and add that to your report."

A report. His mother thought he would draw up a report on his grandmother's living conditions and value her house. To shift her into a care home. She was utterly deluded. "Sure."

"You'll call me and keep me in the loop?"

"Sure."

"I'll look forward to it."

She hung up.

Jake had no intention of doing any of the things his mother demanded. But it was always easier to say 'sure' and disappoint by not following through than to have a fight. All confrontations were better done face to face. Alison could argue for hours when her faceless opponent was on the other end of a telephone.

He drained his coffee. Rotated his chair back from the view of the city to the pile of papers on his desk.

Chapter Three

"Have you time for a cup of tea?"

There was something bothering Eleanore. Evie knew her neighbour well enough to spot the little trace of a frown on her forehead, to hear the different tone in her voice.

"I certainly do." Evie lifted the plastic bag in her hand. "I picked you up a coffee cake because book club is at your house tonight, isn't it?"

"It is. Thank you, dear."

Evie followed Eleanore into the kitchen. There was one comfortable padded chair next to the Aga, and as usual, Cleo was curled up on it.

Evie gave Eleanore side eyes. "You should sit on your comfortable chair and let her sit on the cushion on the kitchen chair."

"She just jumped up there when I went to open the door." She hesitated. Considered. Then grinned. "Okay, I lie. She's been there all afternoon." She stroked the cat's head. "I love seeing her curled up like that. She puts a paw over her eyes. It's very sweet."

Evie couldn't scold Eleanore for something she did herself. "Will I make the tea?"

"Yes, do." Eleanore sank onto her regular spot at the head of the table. "Bring plates for the cake, too. There'll still be plenty left for the book club gang."

Once they were settled with large mugs of tea and slabs of coffee cake before them, Eleanore spoke. "I'll really miss Cleo when you move."

"I know." Worry churned in Evie's stomach. "We'll both miss you."

"Any luck?"

Evie had called three more properties that day.

"None of them allow pets." She blew out a breath. "I need to stay in the city because of my job, but there's no way I can live without Cleo." Her mouth tightened. There were only two things she'd inherited from her late mother. Cleo, and her mother's harp. Letting either of them go wasn't an option.

"She could stay here."

Evie's heart tightened. Cleo would be happy with Eleanore, but the thought of being parted hurt like a lance to the chest. Her feelings must have shown on her face, because Eleanore's eyes widened.

"Oh, I'm not trying to steal your cat! Oh pet, don't think that!" She grabbed Evie's hand. "I was wondering if you'd both like to come and live here with me. There's way too much room here for just me. You could have your own floor."

"You—"

"We would have to draw up an agreement, of course. A home share agreement. Felix has a student living with him in a home share and it works great for both parties. You get somewhere to live at a reasonable rent, and I get some money and the benefit of sharing my home and having someone close at hand in case I need help at any stage."

She pulled a face. "Not that I need help, but you know some people might be worried I was getting old."

"Some people?"

The veins on Eleanore's neck stood out like sinewy cables. Her mouth pursed, as though sucking on a lemon. "My daughter." She huffed. "I don't hear from Alison from one month to the next, and then she calls and starts making demands." She swallowed a mouthful of tea. "I'm sorry, dear, you don't want to hear my woes."

"We're friends. We share stuff." Evie picked a fat crumb of cake from the corner of her plate and ate it. "What did she say?"

"The mother of a friend of hers had to go to hospital. She couldn't cope on her own. And of course, Alison started thinking that could have been me. She said I must be getting frail. If she wants to know how frail I am, why doesn't she get on a plane and visit?" She shook her head. "I don't want her to visit. But I *resent* the implication that just because I've reached a certain age, I'm past it."

Evie poured more tea. "You have a better social life than I do." She wasn't just saying it. Eleanore had many friends and seemed to be busy most evenings. She started counting off on her fingers. "Book club, cinema girls, don't you give knitting classes on Wednesdays—"

Eleanore nodded. "Twice a month normally with the knitting rather than every week. Poker every Saturday night at Felix's. Chair yoga, pilates, and the John Woo appreciation society."

Evie blinked.

"He's a master of the genre." There was a touch of defensiveness in Eleanore's proclamation.

"You don't need to persuade me. I love his movies."

"I don't need looking after." Eleanore's eyes flashed. "But I suppose I can't blame Alison for worrying."

There was an air of vulnerability about Eleanore. Despite her steely determination to reject her daughter's concern, if her daughter decided to pressure her into selling her house, she might find herself being railroaded.

Eleanore's mouth flattened into a thin line. "It's my fault. I told her three houses on the road were for sale. That might have started her thinking."

"Why don't you call Felix and get the name of his lawyer who drew up the home share documentation?"

"Felix is coming over tonight. I'll ask him to bring over a copy. You could come over and talk to Felix—oh, no, maybe not."

Her gaze darted to a book face down on the side table.

"Book club is on, and we've been reading Bob Woodward's latest. That's likely to be quite a heated meeting."

Evie finished her tea. "How about you show me around upstairs?"

"Do you think it will work?" Eleanore slowly stood. "Moving in here with me?"

Evie never anticipated having an octogenarian flatmate, but on reflection, she couldn't imagine anyone she'd enjoy living with more. Being a friend and next-door neighbour was quite different than living in close quarters day after day. But her options were non-existent, and the clock was ticking.

She answered honestly. "I don't know, but I'm intrigued by the possibility."

In over a week, Jake had still not managed to carve out enough time to visit his grandmother. The paperwork was more challenging than expected. Sean, the financial controller, was pleasant and efficient, but measured and cautious in what he said. And Cormac Sweeney had still not returned to the office.

There was more going on here than met the eye. He needed someone else's insight as to what that might be.

Jake called his colleague Pat Wiley. Her training as a public relations specialist had earned her a top spot at the company. Her nickname was 'first contact' as she was the first member of Global potential clients would meet. She was warm and friendly. The welcoming human face of a giant corporation.

"Jake, great to hear from you. How's it going?"

"Not great." There was no need to sugar-coat anything with Pat. They'd discussed all the potential challenges that could come up in the acquisitions process. Even when management was keen to cede control in theory, in practice there was bound to be resistance.

"Is it the financials?"

"Not the financials."

"Shit." Pat blew out a breath. "So, it's personnel."

"Yes." The louvre blinds shielded his office partially from view, but he could still see people walking past, carrying cups of coffee from the canteen and sheaves of paper back and forth from the photocopier.

This room was soundproof. He'd checked.

And he'd been polite, but not welcoming. No one would disturb him without careful consideration and knocking first.

"You met with both Matt and Cormac, didn't you?" Pat had been involved in the preliminary discussions with Sweeney Brothers Ltd. If the brothers weren't in agreement about selling the family business, she would surely have picked up on it.

"Christopher and I took them to dinner. They were both charming."

"Christopher?" Jake rubbed the headache forming at his temples. No one had told him Christopher Jones had accompanied Pat on her visit to Ireland. It was unusual for his boss to get involved with any individual acquisition, especially at the very early stages.

"Word came down from high. Brookman wanted Christopher's take on the Sweeney brothers. He is extremely keen to acquire their tech. He was tipped off about their potential by one of his contacts at the Top 500 conference last month and decided he wanted to bring them into the Global family."

Ben Brookman. Global's head honcho and CEO. A legendary elusive figure, so aloof he was positively ephemeral.

"I should have been informed that Christopher had attended that meeting. No one has mentioned meeting him, but if they had...I need to be kept informed of these things."

"I'm sorry. I presumed Christopher had told you."

Pat sounded genuinely sorry. And she was right. The onus was on his direct boss to pass on that information. It must be an oversight. Christopher was mere months from retirement, after which Jake would step up to replace him.

"So, you and Christopher instigated discussions with Matt?"

"Yes. I judged him to be good at public speaking and skilled at motivating people. The staff I met seemed to like him. Cormac was quiet. He works behind the scenes, but his technical expertise is the core of the business. How did they appear to you?"

"I agree about Matt. I'm concerned I haven't yet met Cormac. Apparently, he has flu. Documentation has been forwarded to him in his sickbed by his request, but he's unavailable for phone calls and emails."

"Okay, there could be a problem, but maybe not. I think we can give him the benefit of the doubt. Unless there's something more that you're not telling me?"

"No, nothing."

"It's only our second attempt to acquire an Irish company, and I know you're burned by previous experience. There's not enough evidence to presume Sweeney Brothers are like Edjicore. Christopher says Sweeney Brothers are an important acquisition that must go ahead."

Jake frowned.

"For the moment then, we'll presume the flu is kicking Cormac's ass, and he's pouring all his strength into recovery." Jake hadn't been sick for well over a year. But if this was his company being acquired, he'd have dragged himself onto a chair and taken a

Zoom meeting. Hell, he'd be emailing from bed, even if he were close to death.

Work hard. Play hard.

"I have someone on the other line. Let's talk Monday." Pat was all efficiency.

"Have a good weekend."

"You too. Take time off and get out there and see the city."

Jake flicked off the light, grabbed his jacket from the back of the chair, and headed out.

Chapter Four

Nicholas Cage and John Travolta have totally different body shapes. But the members of the John Woo Appreciation Society didn't seem to care. And Evie sure wasn't going to be the boring pedant who pointed that out.

"Face/Off is a classic, isn't it?" Rita stage-whispered from her left.

"Sure is."

Rita lived two doors down. They'd walked past each other on numerous occasions during the time Evie had lived on the road but never spoken. She and Eleanore were best friends and founding members of the John Woo Appreciation Society.

Evie had wrangled the previous day off and had started the tortuous process of moving her things across the couple of hundred yards between the two properties. She'd helped drag Soo's possessions into Alex's van two weeks ago. And was more than ready to request that her ex-flatmate returned the favour. They'd been in awe at Alex's box-shifting ability. Well, Evie had been in awe of that. Soo was more impressed with the shift of her boyfriend's muscles under his T-shirt as he hefted heavy boxes.

Having to move had changed both of their lives. Soo and Alex had decided to take their relationship to the next stage. Evie couldn't be happier for them. But why, oh why had they chosen this weekend to go surfing at the coast? Just when she needed them?

After two days of lugging possessions from one house to another, she was worn out. Boxes were stacked in the hall and in the front sitting room. She really should drag them all up upstairs, but her arms were aching and her back hurt. So, when Eleanore had handed her a black T-shirt which was mandatory wear for members of the society, and demanded she shower and join them for their latest bingefest, she had gratefully accepted.

"More popcorn?"

A chorus of yeses.

Evie picked up the large empty bowls from the coffee table and carried them into the kitchen.

When the doorbell rang, she called "I'll get it!" into the darkened room and strode to open the front door wide.

"You!" Instinctively she started shutting the door. But a tanned forearm blocked it, bracketing her body.

The man was close. So close she could see the little flecks of gold in the sea blue of his eyes. This must be some twisted revenge for the coffee splash. Maybe he'd spent the entire week tracking her to her home.

Whatever his motives, he wasn't getting inside the house.

She took a step forward. Sucked in a shaky breath as she collided with a solid mass of muscle. His hand dropped to his side, and then she pulled the door closed behind them.

"What the hell?" The man shoved a hand through his chocolate brown hair, mussing it. He was dressed casually in a blue shirt open at the neck and a pair of jeans that looked suspiciously as if they'd been pressed.

"It was an accident. The company is sorry about your shirt. They'll replace it if you need that to happen." Despite Oscar's throwaway comment, there was no way the company would replace his shirt, but if it got him off the doorstep, she'd buy him one herself.

A dawning expression appeared on his face. His eyes, which up until now had been squinting at her with suspicion, widened as he examined her features with a laser focus.

"You drive that bloody yellow thing."

"It's called a Duck."

He looked as though he'd only just put it together. Which was ridiculous, because if he didn't know she lived here—

"You think I'm here for you?" His mouth twisted in a not-in-your-wildest-dreams way. *Insulting*.

"You're not?" She crossed her arms.

A lazy smile curved his lips. "Well, I could be." His gaze flickered down to her chest. "Woo hoo."

Every member of the society wore the same T-shirt. Eleanore had been browsing the internet and seen them. *Woo hoo!* scrawled on the front with the immortal line, *What a ride*, written below. She'd bought extras for new recruits.

"What does that say underneath?" He peered closer.

She slapped his chest.

"Never you mind."

His gaze locked with hers.

"If you're not here for me, who are you here for?" *Got him*.

She probably looked smug. She sure felt smug. Let him talk his way out of this one.

"I'm here..." He held out a bunch of flowers that he'd been holding that she hadn't noticed up till now. "To see Eleanore."

The smile slid right off Evie's face like butter off hot toast. "You're here for Eleanore?"

Her mind was going everywhere, all at once. Imaging a world where the hot guy she'd been daydreaming about was dating her roommate. Flitting through a montage of colliding with a near nude him coming out of the bathroom wrapped in a towel. Awkward breakfast conversation.

When Eleanore had reeled off her hobbies, she's neglected to mention...

Start at the beginning.

"What's your name?"

"Jake."

She couldn't place his name. In fact, she was convinced she'd never heard Eleanore speak of a Jake before.

"Jake Ridley. Eleanore's one and only grandson."

The brunette's mouth opened and closed, without any sound issuing forth.

"And you are?"

"Evie," she whispered. "You better come in."

She fished a bunch of keys from the back pocket of her jeans and unlocked the door. "Mind the boxes."

He followed her into the dimly lit hallway.

It was just as he remembered. The floor was patterned with black, white, and terracotta red floor tiles, the walls a pale tobacco buff, which might once have been white. A brass lantern hung overhead. When the early morning sun hit the front of the house, there would be a mosaic of colour painted on the floor from the stained-glass panels in two narrow windows on each side of the door.

At night, the lantern's glow would change the mood in the hall again, making it warm. Making it feel like home. The tall brass cylinder holding walking sticks was still there. He bet if he searched, he'd find the one he'd found on one of his and Gran's walks in the country. It had been nothing, just an old stick with a bulbous lump on the end. His mother had tried to throw it out, but he'd gripped onto it for dear life, so she'd had no option but to relent.

Eleanore had pulled out a shillelagh from the stick box. She'd held it against Jake's smaller stick and compared the two. She'd declared them the same, except for the colour; her older shillelagh was glossy black.

"It is Jake's shillelagh. It shall live here." Tone brooking no argument, she'd slotted it into the cylinder. Then she'd placed an arm around Jake's shoulders and hugged him tight.

Everything was familiar. Even the faded Polaroids in wooden frames.

Evie had stopped next to a door. She placed a finger on her lips and pointed into the kitchen. When he walked in, she closed the door behind them.

"What's going on?" He heard voices in the other room. And what sounded like the television cranked up to max. Either that or there was a war going on next door.

"They're in the middle of watching a movie." She sank onto a chair.

"I think seeing her grandson will beat watching television—"

"Wait. Sit for a minute."

She wasn't exactly pleading, but there was an edge to her tone, as though she had more to say she needed him to hear.

He pulled out the old kitchen chair and sat.

"Obviously, if she were alone in there, she'd flick off the television and transfer all her attention to you. But she's not." She waved at her chest. "This T-shirt which she gave me to wear, incidentally, is the uniform of the John Woo Appreciation Society. Ten members of which are having their meeting."

It made no sense.

"They all love John Woo movies." She caught a look at the bowls and popcorn abandoned on the table. "I was making more popcorn when you rang."

She stood and emptied the packets of microwave popcorn into the bowls. "Let me just deliver these, then I'll be back."

She rushed out. When she pushed open the door to the living

room, the sound level kicked up a notch. And after a couple of minutes, she was back.

"How much longer does the movie have to run?"

"Travolta is closing in on Nicolas Cage. There's the big shootout yet to come…"

She took one look at his face. "Oops, spoilers."

"I'd have to be living under a rock to have missed it."

"Eleanore loves it so much. You must have seen it a million times." She beamed as if he must know it was his grandmother's favourite film. But he didn't. If anyone had asked, he would have guessed some period drama or something.

At a loss as to what to say to deflect from his grandmother's favourite anythings, he said the first thing that came to mind. "Why are the society all here watching it?"

A look of faint puzzlement altered her features. "Well, because she's the president. The co-founder. And Rita's not up for hosting."

Rita?

"Look. If you go in there now, it'll be a whole thing. She'll have to rush you out of the room so as not to disturb the screening, and she'll be distracted. Can you wait ten or fifteen minutes until the movie is done? The meeting happened before the film, so they'll all be on their way once the titles have rolled."

"Okay. Sure."

Her face brightened. "Great. Coffee?"

She bustled about, totally familiar with the layout of the kitchen. Lifting two mugs from the cupboard above the sink, flicking on the kettle, and taking milk from the fridge.

"So, you live here."

"I do." She placed a coffee in front of him. "Well, I will, once I've finished moving everything in." A deep dimple creased her cheek as she smiled. "You may have noticed the boxes. I've spent all day dragging things in. And have yet to carry them upstairs."

So, this was new. He imagined if Alison knew anything about this new development, she'd have passed it on immediately.

"I used to live next door." She pointed out the window where a large *for sale* sign was planted in the front garden of the house next door. "But they gave me notice, and Eleanore asked me to move in."

"She asked you—"

"Well, mostly she asked Cleopatra."

He frowned.

"She's my cat. You know what cats are like. She spends half the time over here anyway, hanging with Eleanore. Anyway, she didn't want Cleo moving away, and..."

Her voice trailed off. She leant forward and placed her forearms on the table. Examined his face. "Why are you frowning?"

An opportunist was in the process of taking advantage of his grandmother, and he was supposed to grin and bear it? Not likely. But he flattened out his expression to neutral. It wouldn't do to tip her off to his next moves.

"I'm just surprised." He sipped his coffee.

Chapter Five

He was trying for nonchalant, but there had been a trace of suspicion in his gaze when she told him she'd moved in with his grandmother. He'd done quite a good job of hiding it, but she was used to reading expressions and micro changes in body language. It had been a useful skill growing up. Her mother's illness had forced Evie to take on the role of grown-up way before she'd finished school.

Every day after school she cleaned the house, made dinner, and helped her mother organise the bills, putting the 'must pay's' in one pile and the ones that could be delayed in another.

Even with the disability benefit, they'd had to watch every cent. At one stage, they'd even considered selling the harp. But the ache at the thought of music leaving their lives—that final acknowledgment that her mother's career was well and truly over, cut deep.

Bright side out.

Even when she'd been young and things had been easy, that had been her mother's favourite saying. A motto she lived by. She'd lived her life in optimism, hope, and positivity. Evie was determined to follow her example. But that didn't mean she was oblivious. There was no doubt that Jake was both wary and suspicious.

She propped her elbows on the table. Tilted her head and fixed her gaze on him. "So, tell me about *you*, Jake. You're not from around here?"

There wasn't even a hint of brogue in his English accent.

His eyes narrowed a little. "No. I live in the UK."

"Just a quick visit to see Granny then?"

He checked the empty microwave popcorn bag absently. "No, I've been here a week, and will be here for quite a while. I'm working with a company around the corner."

His words sparked a load of questions. What company around the corner? What did he work at? And if he'd been working so close by, why on earth hadn't he visited earlier?

"I've been busy."

He glanced at a polished steel watch on his wrist. "Will they be much longer?"

He was a good-looking guy, but he sure could do with some pointers on how to win friends and influence people.

Before she had a chance to formulate a snappy comeback, there was a roar from the next room. Followed by a lot of clapping.

"It's over." She walked to the door. Stopped, and cast a gaze back to where he still sat at the kitchen table. "Are you coming then?"

Eleanore had never mentioned him. But when Jake followed her into the room, the look on Eleanore's face was of pure joy.

It was as though a light had been turned on inside her. Her skin warmed with an inner glow, and a wide smile transformed her face the moment she recognised him.

She didn't bother with words. There was no need when her body language was screaming at him to come close into her wide-open arms. He crossed the room in a couple of long strides. She was standing by the time he made it to her side, and then they were locked in an embrace. In a warm, real connection of two people long parted who cared about each other and needed to show it.

The pure and honest emotion evident in their greeting made

Evie feel voyeuristic, but she couldn't look away. An ache in her chest, like someone twisting and turning her muscles inside, made her rub her chest with her clenched palm.

The last time she'd felt the clench was when she'd been waiting at arrivals at the airport for a friend. People watching, she'd seen the whole gamut of emotions flicker across the faces of those waiting. The constant checking of the arrivals board. Glances at their phone, to check they hadn't missed a message. The squint and frown as they calculated the time the plane had landed, added on time for retrieving a suitcase, and then the long trek to the terminal building.

The hope every time the automatic glass doors parted.

Searching the faces, looking for their loved ones.

And the unadulterated joy of first catching sight of that special person. Evie'd had to blink back threatened tears as the rush of second-hand emotion blasted across the space between her and the reuniting couple or family.

She didn't have anyone anymore.

She'd averted her eyes. Pulled in a breath and released it slowly.

Then when she'd looked up again, it was to see her friend wave and walk in her direction. They'd greeted each other with smiles and warmth, but without that heart breaking clutch of hearts and welling emotion.

It was an airport pickup. Not a meeting of souls.

Jake took a step away.

Eleanore reached up to touch his face. And left it there, as she stared into his eyes.

Evie thought she knew her neighbour. All the important things about her life, anyway. When she and Jake had spoken in the kitchen earlier, it had been obvious he didn't keep up with events in his grandmother's life. He nodded politely when she spoke of her friends, but he'd given the impression he was a visitor in Eleanore's life, rather than an integral part.

The vignette before her illustrated otherwise. He may not

31

know the day to day, but Jake and Eleanore shared a deep and true connection. They didn't need an outsider intruding.

Evie turned and walked back into the kitchen.

Eleanore's warm hand rested on Jake's cheek. She gazed at him in the way she always had. As though he was the most interesting person in the world. As though there was nothing more important than to make that connection.

Surprise had stolen her words. But not for long.

She patted his shoulder.

Took a deep breath.

And then there was no stopping her. "What are you doing here?"

Before he could answer...

"You've got very thin. Are you taking care of yourself?"

"When did you get here? How long are you visiting for?"

He opened his mouth to speak, but she kept talking, so he closed it again.

"Are you just here for the day, or are you staying?" She glanced behind him. "Have you a suitcase?"

She blinked, as though finally registering that everyone else had left and they were alone. "Did you get to meet any of my friends? And how about Evie? Did you meet Evie?"

She peered around him. "Where is Evie?"

She stopped for a breath.

He smiled. Said nothing for a long moment until she realised.

"I haven't let you get a word in edgewise, have I?"

He nodded.

"Where's Evie?"

Of all the questions she'd asked, that was the one she chose to repeat. That was the one that was of most importance to her.

Whoever Evie was, however their relationship had developed, she was an important person in Eleanore's life.

Evie had faded away at their reunion, but he hadn't heard the front door open.

"I think she's in the kitchen." He placed a hand on Eleanore's arm and steered her down to sitting again. "I'll get her in a minute. First, let's catch up."

Eleanore agreed.

He answered all her questions. "I'm here on business. I anticipate I'll be here for a few weeks, maybe longer."

That wasn't exactly the truth. He had planned a precise time frame for dealing with the Sweeney Brothers situation, with no wriggle room. But he had a lot of holiday time accruing. Once this assignment was over, he could afford to spend some here with his grandmother.

Christopher was the head of Global Innovations in England. He had announced his intention to retire six months ago and had recommended Jake as his successor.

A position Jake wasn't sure he wanted. The salary and perks were off the charts, but it was still someone else's company, not his own venture. And there were certain policies Global espoused that Jake objected to.

"My suitcase is back in my hotel room. I didn't meet your friends. I've met Evie."

She looked him up and down.

"And no, I haven't lost weight. I eat just fine. So, tell me. What's the story with you and Evie?"

He paid close attention as she explained how she'd offered a home to Evie and her cat. She rambled about her friend Felix and how his successful home share arrangement had inspired her to investigate further.

"There's no third party involved, overseeing things?"

Eleanore scoffed. "There's no need for that. I have a copy of the contract Felix and his solicitor drew up, and I thought we'd just go with that." Jake made a mental note to get his legal team to review the paperwork and make sure every eventuality was covered.

"Neither of you have signed anything yet?"

"No." She made a squeaking noise, and Evie's cat shot across the room and dived into her lap. "We decided to try living together for a month first to make sure we're compatible." She chucked the cat under its chin. "But we all get on great, don't we, Cleo?"

"Is she paying you rent?"

Eleanore fixed him with a frown, as though he'd muttered a dirty word. "Of course. She insisted. Because we haven't started the agreement yet, she just put the same amount she's paying next door into an envelope, and I wrote her a receipt for a month's rent."

Evie might share his grandmother's home, but it wasn't as clear cut as a regular rental. She was potentially in a powerful position over someone who might be considered vulnerable. He had never seen Eleanore as vulnerable, but his mother, Alison, did. She'd wanted him to evaluate Eleanore's ability to continue living alone.

He had a responsibility to make sure that this new person who had become an important addition to Eleanore's life was trustworthy and capable.

"What do you mean, your suitcase is at your hotel?"

Eleanore cherry picked his answers to the statement that interested her.

The change of subject jerked him out of his thoughts. He stared at her blankly.

"You can't stay in a hotel. You must move in here. Your old bedroom is just as you left it."

The hotel had fast Wi-Fi, a laundry service, twenty-four-hour room service, and a power shower that pinned him to the wall with a blast of steaming water.

"I'll check out tomorrow morning."

Chapter Six

Evie staggered into Soo's new apartment and collapsed on the sofa. Her face was red and her body sweaty. Three weeks into salsa workout classes, and she was still floundering.

"You keep telling me I'll find my natural rhythm, but what if I don't have any natural rhythm? Huh?" She loved to dance. There was nothing like the freedom of letting go and shaking her ass on the dance floor. But synchronised dancing—doing the same thing as her friends at the same time and in the same way—seemed to be a skill she was yet to master.

"It'll come." Soo pulled open the door of her massive fridge and peered inside. "Water? Juice? Vodka tonic?"

"You have to ask?" Evie shifted to sitting. "But maybe we should have water as well to hydrate."

"Come and help me then."

They piled a tray with a couple of glasses each and a large bowl of crisps and sat.

"What time's Alex home?"

He'd seen her and Soo after their exercise classes before. Salsa

35

dancing having been preceded by a three-month stint of line dancing and before that, power Pilates.

There had been no embarrassment as they debated sticking Post-its on the toes of Evie's cowboy boots with *left* and *right* on them in an attempt to make her turn the same direction as the rest of the class as sexyhip Bradley led from the front.

But things were different now. She couldn't shower and disappear to bed to watch Netflix. She was a visitor in their home.

"Alex won't be back for ages." Soo leant back on the cushions. "He's out with some work mates and told me he'd grab something to eat with them so not to wait for him. I thought we could have pizza and you can stay the night. Test out the spare room." There was compassionate affection in Soo's tone, caring in the depths of her eyes. The sale of the house had changed everything for both of them.

For her, the change had been positive. The house going on the market had forced her and Alex to consider their future and decide to move in together.

Soo was one of the only people who knew how alone Evie was.

And that the loss of her home and the constant company of her friend was a body blow. One she was well able to survive, but tough, nonetheless.

"Thanks, hon. I'll stay for pizza, but then I'm heading home."

Soo tilted her head to the side and observed Evie, assessing. "How are you doing?"

Evie's skin prickled. The urge to push her friend away, to demonstrate that she was unaffected, that she didn't need anyone's help, was overwhelming.

"It's okay. Everything is fine."

Soo's eyebrow rose a fraction. "It must be different, living with Eleanore."

"It's not just Eleanore." She tugged at her sleeve, twisting it around her wrist.

"Oh yes! The grandson!" Soo's gaze sharpened, and she leant

forward. "I forgot about him. What's he like?" They'd spent an hour texting back and forth once Jake moved in.

"He's infuriating." This morning he'd dashed into the bathroom moments before she'd planned to and had used almost all the hot water, reducing her shower to a quick wash and cold rinse of her shampooed head. "He drank all the coffee."

"All?"

"I made a jug. For me. He just presumed it was there for the taking."

The corner of Soo's mouth twitched. "You could share." She grinned. "I know you don't like to share your supply of coffee, but you used to let me have a cup when we lived together."

"Only after we'd become friends. And I always made extra. Yesterday I'd made a half jug. One cup before getting out of bed, one for after the shower, and half a cup while checking headlines on my phone. He stole one of my cups."

She was pouting. And didn't feel bad about it. The way he'd strode across the kitchen and helped himself to a cup without even asking rankled.

"I have no idea how long he plans to stay, either. Eleanore and I agreed that I would have three rooms on the first floor. A bedroom, bathroom, and a room that I can convert into a sitting room. We share the kitchen. Eleanore had to move her bedroom downstairs last year and converted the dining room. Jake is staying in the remaining bedroom on that floor, and we're sharing the bathroom."

Soo sloshed more vodka into Evie's glass and topped it up with some tonic. "It's temporary."

Evie had told her everything about their original meeting. Including how attractive she'd found him. "It's been over a year since Wyatt. And you said Jake was good looking, so how bad can living with a hot, single guy be?"

"He's not my type."

Both eyebrows rose.

"He's not." There was an unexpected heat in Evie's cheeks. "He works too hard, and he's too curious. He tries to make conversation, but behind it all I get the impression he's probing for information. He asked me about what my parents do, and where I grew up."

"Cold-hearted bastard." Soo's eyes twinkled. "Seriously, though, Evie. Some people might call that flirting, rather than grilling."

"I don't."

"You don't because you're prickly as fuck." Soo stated blandly. "You get in your head too much. There's nothing wrong with sharing some details of your life with people." She held up a hand to stop Evie interrupting.

"I know. I know. You hate being pitied for having no parents. You don't want tragedy to define you. But by closing yourself off, you're pushing people away. Everyone has pain in their life. And if they haven't experienced it yet, it's only a matter of time before they find themselves engulfed."

"So I should cut the tall, dark, and handsome stranger I'm living with some slack?"

"You should."

"Do you have a lint roller?" Yes, Jake wasn't wearing his trousers. But his black jersey boxers were perfectly decent, so there was no reason for Evie to be staring at his legs as if he was auditioning for *Magic Mike.*

She didn't seem to be able to form words.

"A lint roller." He held up his black trousers. "As the owner of a cat with a shedding problem, you must have one."

He checked his watch. Damn, he was going to be late.

"I don't." Her eyes narrowed as she saw the furry mark on his crotch. "But I have duct tape."

Jake bit back a sarcastic comment. His bare foot tapped on the ground as she rooted around in a cardboard box next to the kitchen dresser.

"You should really move that box. It's in the way."

She shot him a glare.

He shouldn't antagonise her. There really wasn't time. And she was finding him something to clean the fur from his trousers. But sometimes it was just so easy to get a reaction that he couldn't resist.

"Here." She held up a battered roll. "Rip off a strip," she said as she did. "Fold it over on itself, then wrap it around your knuckles —" She held out her other hand.

He obediently handed over his trousers.

She checked out his underwear again. And blushed as he noticed her looking.

"Roll it over." She rolled the sticky side of the tape over the fabric, peeling off a layer of Cleopatra's thick fur as she did so. "Voila!"

She smiled. There was a slight gap between her front teeth, and one side of her mouth lifted a tiny fraction higher than the other. Attraction stirred.

"Busy day?"

He crossed his arms. "Big meeting." The way her hands moved over the fabric was mesmerising.

"You've been working a lot." She looked up. "Eleanore thinks you work too hard."

"I know. She's told me."

Evie handed over his trousers, and he stepped into them. As he fastened the button and zipped up the fly, it struck him that maybe this was the first time he'd put on his clothes in front of a fully dressed woman. He'd undressed before many.

This was the sort of thing a married couple might do. Have a conversation while one of them dressed. With the emphasis being on what they were talking about.

It felt natural. And it felt good.

"Would you like to join me, Eleanore, and Felix for dinner later? I'm making fajitas and could do with some help fixing the mojitos."

"I'm sorry. I think I'll be working late. I'll grab something at my desk."

There seemed to be an always swirling carousel of friends rotating into Eleanore's orbit. He loved his grandmother dearly but had no time to get swept up in her endless social whirl.

"You're always making dinner. I'm sure that's not part of any agreement that you have to cook for Eleanore."

She gave him a withering look. "Sometimes I cook, and sometimes she does. It's called living together. As a member of the household, you're always welcome to join. Or to volunteer to cook. If you can. Otherwise, I'm sure your grandmother will be happy to give you lessons."

"I eat out. Or order in. There's an Italian restaurant on the corner. I'll pop in tomorrow and pick up a menu, and we can dial a meal in when you're both free."

"Fair enough." She scratched her neck. "Do you never cook, though? I've never seen you make anything except cereal."

"I have an oven in my apartment." He hoped she wouldn't question him further. Because having to admit that he stored his winter sweaters in the oven because of lack of wardrobe space probably wouldn't help his case any.

"What's happening at work? Are there problems?"

He tucked in his shirt, buttoned his cuffs.

"Cormac Sweeney has been avoiding me. I can't get a bead on him. And his brother seems to think I'm a heartless devil intent on slashing their company to ribbons." He blew out a frustrated breath. "If I could get them away from the other employees, get them into a relaxed atmosphere, and break through the barriers I'm sure we could have a breakthrough."

"Take them for dinner, maybe?"

"Matt took me home for dinner the first week I was here. His wife is great. Having her in the mix made things much, much easier. She diffused tensions and made the whole thing more casual. Today is the first time Cormac has agreed to give me some of his undivided attention, and I'd love to build on that."

He ran a hand through his hair.

Pat had found the Sweeney brothers charming. They'd been much more relaxed in the presence of a woman than they were likely to be with him. An idea bloomed.

"Hey, I don't suppose you'd help me out by joining me for a business dinner, would you?"

Evie grinned. "Are you asking me on a date?"

Asking Evie on a date wasn't a half bad idea. But if he did, neither of the Sweeney brothers would be tagging along.

"I'd be very grateful."

Her lips were full and pink. Why was he suddenly noticing?

"Very grateful." He leant closer into her personal space.

"Grateful enough to carry my mother's harp upstairs?"

"Even that grateful."

She stood. "In that case, you're on. I'll go on a date with you. Any night but Friday. Friday is movie night."

Eleanore had presented with him with one of the Woo Hoo T-shirts that morning. He'd been amused to see the line of text under the headline that Evie had crossed her arms over on their first meeting.

"I remember. What a ride."

Chapter Seven

Early Thursday evening, Jake rapped on Evie's bedroom door. He'd tried to get to know her better since they made the dinner date, but she was slippery as a bar of soap in the shower when it came to personal questions. What he knew about her background would fit on the back of a stamp.

All seemed good on the surface. She paid rent and bought groceries. She socialised with Eleanore's crowd some nights and with her friend Soo on others. She might be Eleanore's perfect home share person, but he couldn't be sure. Because Evie kept him at arm's length. She had an opinion about everything unimportant. A wisecracking return to all his lobbies. But when he asked her anything real, she retreated into her shell like a threatened hermit crab.

He needed to know her better.

Dinner tonight would accomplish two things. First, it would provide a relaxed atmosphere to thaw the ice with Cormac. Second, it would give him a chance to connect with Evie without Eleanore in the way.

He rapped again.

"It's not a—" Evie jerked the door open. She was wrapped in a towel, and her hair was damp. Half was dead straight, the other half in curls like a mermaid or a country music singer. "Jake. You're early."

"I need to talk to you."

She looked him up and down. "Are we still on for the dinner tonight?" A couple of water drops glistened on her arms. She had cute shoulders. He didn't think he'd ever noticed anyone's shoulders in the past. Before he could start to notice anything else about her towel-wrapped body, he stepped back.

"Yes. But we've got some time. I need to talk to you. I'll be in the sitting room."

He bolted downstairs.

He hadn't moved the harp. He'd offered to manoeuvre the unwieldy instrument up the narrow stairway to the first floor, but Evie had said she was only joking. Eleanore was adamant it should stay in pride of place in the sitting room. She said it added elegance and gravitas.

He had to agree.

He trailed a finger over the strings.

The huge harp would dominate the space in any of the rooms upstairs. But here in the stately living room with high, eighteenth-century ceilings and tall sash windows, it looked right at home.

"Don't touch."

Evie stood in the doorway. She'd dressed in the baggiest sweatshirt known to humankind and wore leggings and knockoff crocs. She waved a hand at her hair. "I need to do the other side. I can't go out like this."

"We need to know things about each other."

She looked at him blankly.

"For the date. Because we're supposed to be friends who know stuff about each other."

"Ah." She tapped the side of her head. "My hair's drying. We'll have to do this upstairs. Come on."

He followed her upstairs. As she gathered curling tongs and a comb and plugged the instruments of torture back in, he perched on the end of her bed. Cleo noticed him from her spot next to the radiator and jumped up to sit on his lap.

Jake stroked Cleo, who purred like a speedboat engine. "I like what you've done with the place." It wasn't much. She'd moved out some of the more antiquated furniture and put up artistic photographs of beaches and seas. "The photos are great."

"They're taken by a guy I work with. Oscar loves photography. The company ran an auction last year for charity and I bought the whole series."

"He should consider going out on his own."

Evie twirled a skein of hair around the heated barrel. Counted to five and released a perfect curl. "Easier said than done. He has the talent and the equipment, but starting a business is so challenging."

"Tell me about the harp."

He watched Evie's face in the mirror. She pressed her lips together. This wasn't a subject she wanted to answer.

"The harp belonged to my mother. It's one of the only things I kept." She deftly continued to focus her attention on her hair. "The other is Cleo. She was my mother's cat."

"Do you play?"

A smile touched her lips so fleetingly he might have imagined it. "Once upon a time. I was so curious, you know? Mum made it look so effortless. She played weddings and functions. A lot of her friends were musicians, and she played with many of them. She even sometimes performed in the orchestra. When I was little, there was no money for babysitters, so I used to go with her. She would set me up at the side of the stage, behind the curtain." She smiled a wide smile, taken over by a happy memory.

"I'd forgotten about that. Thanks for reminding me." Her gaze met his in the mirror.

"She used to say it gave her confidence, seeing me there. That she needed to see a little piece of her heart while she played." She finished the curling procedure and pulled the machine from the wall. "She wanted to teach me *Danny Boy*. I wanted to learn something more modern. She taught me a couple of songs, but I haven't felt able to play since she died."

She swivelled on the stool to face him. "What about you? What do I need to know about you? Should we know each other's dating history?"

The story that men never talked about relationships, both in groups of all men together or when they got together with their female friends, was completely untrue. He and his friends spent ninety per cent of their time together talking about disastrous dating adventures.

"I guess."

"You go first." She crossed her arms.

"I've had a few relationships. I shared a flat with one girlfriend a couple of years ago."

"She must have been more than just a girlfriend, then?"

Jake rubbed the back of his neck. He didn't want to talk about his ex. "I think we were both serious about each other for a while. We lived together for eighteen months or so, but things didn't work out." He felt the same lurch of dread he always felt when he allowed himself to think about Polly. Because every time he thought about her, there was a painful ache deep in his chest. He paused, noticing the ache had yet to materialise.

"Why?"

He glared.

"I have to ask. We're supposed to be friends."

"My mother says Polly left me because I wasn't successful enough. I'm the youngest of four overachievers and she's always expected me to be the best at everything." He pulled a face. "Top marks at school. Prefect. Top Boy. Captain of the cricket team. Debating team. She thinks Polly left because I hadn't 'fully reached my potential.'"

Evie visibly flinched. "Ouch. That's harsh. Is your mother

right?" She tilted her head to the side. "If she is, then Polly didn't deserve you." She was warm and supportive. She'd make a great friend if this was real.

"I found her in our bed with her boss." Once, he would have been sliced in two sharing the real reason he and Polly had parted ways. "I haven't told anyone that."

"I won't tell anyone."

He'd told himself he didn't know her. But somehow Jake knew without a doubt that Evie wouldn't betray his confidence.

"Have you any lost loves I should know about?"

"I lived with someone during college. It didn't work out." Her mouth flattened in a straight line.

Someone had hurt her. Conflicting emotions warred within Jake. Anger at the man who'd toyed with her heart. Surprise that he gave a damn. Interest at the thought of romance with this enigmatic woman.

Her phone beeped, drawing her attention. "Oh shit, we have to be there in half an hour." She stood and fluttered her arms at him. "Get out of here and get dressed!"

Jake walked across the hall to his room. Evie had opened up and given him such honest answers, he'd felt compelled to reciprocate.

She'd had lots of ideas about this evening. He'd been happy to listen to all of them. She'd nixed the idea of a fancy restaurant and suggested they make it casual. That the venue should be good food, simply served. That way, the brothers wouldn't have to dress formally and would feel more at ease. She'd even cleverly suggested they choose a place with Irish cuisine so they could teach Jake a few things.

Switching up the dynamic. Upending the status quo.

She'd told him to wear jeans and a shirt open at the neck. Had rifled through his wardrobe and picked out the one shirt that wasn't white he'd shoved into his suitcase at the last moment. He'd packed the black denim on impulse, thinking it would suffice if he needed to do gardening work for Eleanore.

He cinched his black belt. Cast an assessing eye over his black jeans and black denim shirt outfit, and wondered if he was crazy to let Evie determine what he should wear meeting clients.

There was a tap at the door.

When he called 'enter', Evie strode in.

She planted her hands on her hips. She examined him carefully. "You look great."

"So do you." The cherry red dress had thin straps and fell to just below her knee. It was made of some floaty material that skimmed her curves rather than hugging them. The only jewellery she wore was a pair of gold dangly earrings with blood red stones in them. "I thought we were dressing casual?"

"This is casual." She grinned and walked close to check her reflection in the mirror. "Girl casual is different to boy casual."

"Evidently." Their reflections looked good next to each other.

She wore red shoes too. With high heels that brought the top of her head to the level of his mouth. If he leant in, it would be so easy to kiss her.

Their eyes met in the mirror. Time seemed to stop for a moment, suspended in a crystal sphere where all that mattered was the awareness blooming in her eyes.

They stared at their reflection as if they were looking at two strangers. While behind the façade, every inch of Jake was aware of Evie. With every breath, he breathed in her warm, spicy floral perfume. The aura that flowed from her surrounded him in warmth and comfort. They felt like a unit, even though they were nothing of the sort.

"What have you told them about me?" Her voice was breathy, quiet. As though she didn't want to shatter the accord between them.

Jake blinked. "Just that you're a friend." He turned away from the illusion in the mirror.

~

The Sweeney brothers were charming. Matt was entranced by his wife, Lisa, and took every opportunity to show her so. He made sure her glass was always filled, listened when she spoke, and stroked her arm as it rested on the white linen tablecloth between courses.

"Have you been married long?" Evie asked when the men started to talk sports.

"Two years." Lisa cast a loving glance at her husband's profile. "But it feels like we're honeymooners." Her cheeks flushed. "Matt's very romantic. He's throwing a party to celebrate our anniversary. I suggested we do something private, like dinner or a mini break, but he wants a big party."

She fiddled with her napkin. Leant in.

"I'm so glad to meet you. Matt's been so worried that Cormac and Jake weren't gelling. This deal means a lot to us. We want it to go ahead." She rested her elbows on the table and clasped her hands together, effectively hiding her mouth from the men across the table. She spoke quietly. "Cormac." She winced. "I don't want to be telling tales out of school, but—"

Jake's head swivelled. His gaze connected with hers.

"I think I'll visit the ladies room. You coming?" Evie asked.

"Yes." Lisa took the napkin from her lap and placed it on the table. "We'll be back in a second, guys."

Safe in the privacy of the women-only haven, Lisa spilled.

"Cormac doesn't trust people easily. And somehow, he's got it into his head that Jake is cold and cutthroat." Honesty shone from her eyes. "Matt and Cormac started the company and feel a responsibility to everyone who works there. After Global and Sweeney Brothers started negotiations, Cormac saw something on social media that gave him doubts."

Evie didn't know any more than Lisa did about what sort of man Jake was in business. But he was a decent man who cared fiercely for his grandmother. In her gut, she felt he was trustworthy.

"What did he see?"

"Something on Twitter from a company that had been taken over by Global."

Evie nodded as though she knew what Lisa was referring to.

"Anyway, what I want to say is that he must be a good guy if you're dating him." Her soft smile reminded Evie how the engine driving Lisa was love. "You're so down to earth. And driving an amphibious vehicle, that's so amazing. I can tell you now, the guys will be begging for a tour before the night's out!"

"I'll get Jake to set up a date. And you must come too. You'd look cute in a Viking helmet."

Dimples dented Lisa's cheeks. "And you both must come to our anniversary party this Saturday. Cormac had invitations printed, which matched our wedding invites." She rolled her eyes but couldn't hide how touched she was by her husband's romantic gesture.

Jake was settling the bill when they arrived back at the table.

He stood with a smile the moment he saw her. "Ready to go?"

A burble of voices emanated from the sitting room when they entered the house.

Jake reached for something on the table next to the door.

He held it up in front of her face with a disapproving scowl. "This is hardly appropriate."

Evie looked at the book in his hand. She hadn't read it yet, but had planned to carve out a little time in her future to spend with the blue alien with an eight pack on the cover. Strange Jake was so prudish, though.

She rose her eyebrows. "Really?"

"You live with a lady in her eighties. You should keep this in your room."

Evie couldn't hold back a snort. "Uh, well I might. If it were my book." She took it out of his hand and skimmed the back cover copy.

A gale of laughter swept from the room ahead. "Tonight is book night." She held up the book. "And this is the book they're discussing."

Jake peeked around the door, then darted back. "Half of them are men."

"And they're all intelligent, interested people. Ones who aren't repressed. They discuss everything the world has to offer. And I mean everything. Eleanore's friend Maggie asked if she could hold an Ann Summers party here next week. And she said yes."

She leant in. "Monday, six o'clock, if you can get home from work in time." She took off her coat and hung it on one of the mahogany pegs attached to the wall. "Do you want to go in and say hello?"

Jake shook his head. "I have Jameson in my room. Let's just grab some glasses and drink it in your sitting room."

She needed to talk with him and had intimated as much on the taxi ride home. She still hadn't worked out exactly how to explain that they were now in a relationship, but she needed to inform him before tomorrow.

He grabbed the whiskey, and she set up glasses and ice on the coffee table.

"Tonight went great." He poured her a drink and handed it over. Then settled down in her old armchair, which swallowed him up immediately. "Yikes." He struggled out. "I'm sitting next to you."

"Fair enough."

He clinked his glass against hers. "Thanks for all your help. Everyone was much more relaxed with you there." He took a sip. "You and Lisa seemed to be having a good talk."

She gulped a mouthful. "About that." She closed her eyes for a second, then took a deep breath. "Here's the thing. I discovered the problem with Cormac."

Jake rested his elbows on his knees and gave her his full attention. "What?"

"He saw something on Twitter by a company you took over who were unhappy with how they were treated."

"Damn." Jake took out his phone and tapped a message on the screen. "I must get Pat on to this quick. I told Christopher his actions would have repercussions—"

There was a feeling in her chest. Like a rollercoaster diving into her stomach, or a balloon deflating. "It's true then?"

He cast her a glance. Saw something in her eyes that made him pause and then place his cell phone face down on the table.

"I'm high up in the company, but I don't run it." His expression was earnest, honest. "I didn't agree with the way my boss acted with another company we acquired, and I told him so. It won't happen again."

"Can you be sure of that?" She didn't know how he possibly could. He'd just admitted to not having the final say. What was to prevent the same thing happening to Sweeney Brothers?

Jake engulfed her hand in his. "I promise."

He looked so serious she couldn't leave him hanging. "I believe you. I know you're an honourable man."

She wiggled her hand out from under his and grabbed her glass again. Drained it. And told him the truth.

"Lisa thinks we're in a relationship."

Chapter Eight

"Evie's great." Matt Sweeney strolled into Jake's office and sat.

It wasn't a convenient time. Jake was in the middle of a complex numbers analysis. But talking was more important.

"Yes, she is."

He didn't want to lie to Matt and Cormac. But if believing he was a better man because Evie chose him was what it would take, he'd have to go along with it.

Sleep had been elusive the night before. Evie had poured out the whole story without taking a breath. How Lisa had presumed they were a couple, and how Evie had missed the chance to tell her she was wrong. Then the revelation they found him acceptable if he was part of a couple.

Evie would have to be crazy to go along with this charade. But she'd agreed to. And he knew why. She needed somewhere definite to live and was on a month's trial. His grandmother respected his opinion. If he nixed the idea of the home share, Eleanore would take his objections seriously.

Having a woman eager to please because she was vulnerable

left a bad taste in his mouth. But he needed her just as much as she needed him.

Matt dropped a thick cream card onto the desk. "I told Lisa I'd drop in an invitation to our anniversary party."

Jake took it. "Thanks. We'd love to come." Referring to himself in the plural felt strange. "Evie gave me some possible dates and times to join the Splash Tour next week." He handed over a list. "Any of these would work. If you check with Lisa and Cormac and let me know, Evie will set it up."

"How long have you two been together?" Matt's expression was dreamily romantic.

"Oh, not very long."

"She lives with your grandmother, right? Which came first, the relationship with you or the one with your granny?"

The further he veered from the truth, the more likelihood there would be a mistake or an inconsistency between his story and Evie's. Jake stuck as close to the truth as he could.

"She moved in with my grandmother first. We met and started to date soon thereafter."

"We knew you had Irish roots, but not an Irish girlfriend. Are you planning to relocate?"

"We're just taking it one step at a time."

"Well, it's great to see you looking so happy, man." Matt thumped Jake on the shoulder. "You can tell how much you two care just by the way you look at each other." A wide grin accompanied his words. "I'll let you get back to your numbers."

After back-to-back tours, the last thing Evie felt like was clothes shopping. But she didn't have any option. The party was tomorrow, and she didn't have anything to wear.

Scratch that. She had plenty to wear. Just not anything that fitted the theme. Jake had looked as horrified as she must have when they checked the details on the gold edged invitation.

Dress—strictly cream and gold.

"I guess that means for women only."

Evie raised an eyebrow. "Do you want to check?"

Jake made a quick call to the office.

"It means for everyone." He frowned. "How many men do you know who have cream suits lying around?"

She couldn't think of any, apart from Wilde, Hemingway, and Joyce. "I don't know anyone who has a gold suit, either."

This would be a one-shot clothing choice for them both. Neither would dress in cream or gold if they had any other alternative.

Jake insisted he would pay for a dress, shoes, and a matching bag. She agreed.

She spotted him exactly where he'd promised to be. Standing at the gates to St Stephen's Green. Instead of people watching in the sunshine, he was scanning faces and checking the time. When he caught sight of her in the crowd, his expression lightened, and he strode over.

"I've done my research." He took her arm without so much as a hello and started walking down Grafton Street. "We need to be in Brown Thomas."

She stopped dead.

"This is a one-off outfit neither of us is ever going to wear again. We don't need to break the bank." She gestured at the shops lining each side of the street. "Let's try—"

Jake shook his head. "I don't have time, and neither do you. We are guests at this thing, and we have a certain image to project. One that says we're used to dressing designer because money isn't an issue."

Evie swallowed. Money was an issue. Maybe not for him, but she counted every penny. "We can look the part without wasting money." The shop he was steering them towards had an extensive designer section, but also catered to those who didn't need to rob a bank to pay their bill. She would be able to find something perfect.

In ten minutes, Evie had an armful of clothes and three pairs of shoes to try on. She left Jake in the dust and headed for the changing room.

"Would you like me to call your partner?" The store assistant was obviously envisioning a *Pretty Woman* montage moment. One where Evie pranced out of the dressing room dressed in flouncy confections and Jake lounged on a chair looking her up and down and giving her the benefit of his opinion.

"That won't be necessary."

Evie softened her refusal when she looked out at Jake leafing through racks of pale linen. "He needs something to wear, too. Perhaps you could give him a little help?"

Is there anything more appealing than a vulnerable man? Evie tried on six dresses, found two that would be perfect, and narrowed it down to one. She chose a pair of pale gold heels to match, and a cream handbag.

She was trying on sunglasses—because, why not—when the sales assistant sidled up to her again.

"He's really struggling," she confessed in a breathy whisper. "We've narrowed it down to three, but—"

Evie put the Salvatore Ferragamo Rose Gold shades next to her 'to buy' pile. "Okay, I'll come and help."

She settled down on a velvet armchair. Got into character. And called out, "Okay, honey, show me what you've got!"

Even as the words left her mouth, she was reconsidering. He'd been all business today. And by all accounts, was stressed up the wazoo. The last thing she expected was him to throw back the curtain with a flourish and stride out with a big smile on his face.

"I don't know about this one." He leant close and whispered. "Show me what you've got? What the hell, Evie?" But his eyes glinted with humour.

The pale linen fitted him perfectly. "What's your issue?"

"Well, first it creases."

He pointed at a few micro creases at the top of the legs.

"And I think it's see-through." He lifted up the back of the jacket and peered at his back view.

Which meant she had to stop looking at his crotch and examine his perfect ass.

"Are you wearing black underwear?" As his girlfriend, maybe she was supposed to know the answer to that question. The shop assistant had obviously had enough. She sidestepped to the counter and retrieved a bottle of water and took a deep drink.

"I think you've embarrassed Jane."

She double took so quick whiplash was a possibility. "Jane?"

"Jane." He waved over to the assistant who was talking to another customer. "Jane who's helping."

He knew the name of the sales assistant. And he was concerned about showing his pants in public. Jake Ridley wasn't at all the man she'd thought him.

"And yes, I'm wearing black underwear."

She checked again. "Well, I can't see anything. You're safe. But you're right, linen creases. That's part of its charm."

He frowned. "Not charming."

"Okay." She waved at the dressing room. "Show me the others."

The curtain closed behind him. Jane was suddenly at Evie's side again. "Ask him to wear the Italian suit. He looks fabulous in that one."

Evie walked to the curtain. "Could you try on the Italian suit, honey? Jane says you look great in it."

She looked back to Jane who gave her a double thumbs up.

The shop would be closing soon. Evie rubbed the back of her neck as fatigue bit.

There was the zing of the curtain being pulled back, then Jake stepped out. The Italian suit looked to be a light wool blend. The colour couldn't be described as cream. It was darker, more tawny. He'd added a plain dark gold tie and a brown leather belt.

Evie heard an exhale. And for a moment, she thought she had sighed without realising it. Then she glanced sideways to see Jane looking at Jake misty eyed.

"He looks fabulous," Evie said.

"Totally," Jane agreed.

"Well?" Jake shoved his hands into the pockets. Twisted this way and that in front of the mirror.

"That's the one. Start ringing everything up, Jane."

Chapter Nine

J ake hired a car to drive them out to the party venue, which was a country house hotel nestled in the Wicklow hills. Hotel rooms were available, but it was difficult enough to pass off the date as a business matter with his grandmother without adding a night away into the mix. The driver would pick them up at midnight.

Which suited Jake just fine. The moment they were inside the car, they could stop pretending to be a couple.

Evie looked sensational. The cream silk dress had a deep V in the front and slits up both sides just high enough to show a sexy flash of leg. She accessorised with a wide gold belt and matching shoes with heels that looked like thin solid gold columns. She'd twisted her hair into wavy coils and had fastened a headdress of what looked like golden bay leaves on top.

She looked like a Grecian goddess.

Except for one thing.

When completing their shopping the previous day, he'd noticed the sunglasses she'd placed to one side.

She'd insisted she didn't need them. But he'd seen the way she looked in them. She liked them but wouldn't spend money on such an unnecessary and extravagant purchase.

So, he'd quietly added them to the bill.

And presented them to her just as they climbed into the car.

Goddess in shades.

They pulled up outside the venue. Breckenbridge Hotel had once been a country retreat for a monied family, but now made a decent living as a country house hotel. The cut stone façade was barely visible beneath a blanket of Virginia creeper. The navy-blue front door stood open, inviting guests to enter. There was a shoe scraper to one side of the door, and a water bowl for pets on the other.

It would be a great place for a weekend getaway.

Jake climbed out of the car and walked around to open the door for Evie. She clung onto his arm and gifted him a dazzling smile.

Inside the lobby was a large board with letters stuck on to it.

Sweeney Wedding – Kingfisher Room

And a series of open angle brackets and dashes forming makeshift left pointing arrows.

Evie took off her sunglasses and slipped them into her bag. "Don't leave me alone." She warned. "I might need you."

He'd wanted to talk yesterday after their shopping expedition, but Evie had declared she was too exhausted. Instead, they'd spent this afternoon in her sitting room dreaming up details of how they'd first met, and some significant moments in their made-up relationship.

Hopefully, he wouldn't have to talk about any of it. Lying wasn't in his make-up. He'd never been good at it, even when he was a kid. Whenever there was a breakage in the house, a football through a window, a vase knocked off the table to smash on the polished wooden floor, he was the kid sought out.

Not because he was responsible for the breakage, which he sometimes was, but because he couldn't lie. His mother used to call him closed off and sullen, because his response to interrogation was to clamp his lips closed and avoid looking at his questioner.

If he'd been questioned by the police as a teenager they would have considered him guilty straight away because of his unwillingness to answer questions.

Evie leant in. Someone watching would think she was sharing something personal and intimate. "We should avoid talking about our history as much as possible. No one will want to know anyway. This is Matt and Lisa's day. We just have to look like we're in love."

He brushed back a curling strand of hair from her face. Looked at her mouth. Something in the atmosphere shifted—altered. Awareness narrowed, tuning out the presence of everyone else in the room, sharpening to the woman before him. The woman who was looking at him in a way she hadn't before. As though she wanted to kiss him just as much as he wanted to kiss her.

There was no way in hell she was that good an actress.

His hand lifted of its own volition, and his thumb stroked along her cheek.

Her lips parted a fraction on a sigh.

"Hey, you're here!" Cormac ambled over, one arm out and forward in a welcoming gesture, and the other nursing a pint. He wore an uncharacteristic grin. He thumped Jake on the arm, and kissed Evie on both cheeks. "Come and get a drink." He waved in the direction of the bar. "I'm glad to see you. Matt may be my brother, but we don't hang in the same circles. And to be honest, I'm trying to avoid Lisa's friend who was maid of honour at their wedding. We had a fling, and you know, it didn't exactly end well." He looked down at his cream suit, white shirt, and black tie with disdain. "My mother dragged me out shopping and made me buy this get up. It's got to be the most useless suit I've ever seen. It wrinkles like fuck."

Jake shot Evie a knowing glance. "Yeah, linen does that."

"It's part of its charm," Evie started, but her voice tailed off as both men gave her death stares. "That's what I think anyway," she finished defiantly.

"It cost enough, too. And there's no claiming this back on expenses." He looked bashful, as if he maybe shouldn't be talking about claiming things on expenses with the guy doing a financial deep dive into their company.

"I feel your pain." Jake looked down at his suit. "I'm not a fan of neutral either."

"You both look great." Evie walked up to the bar and accepted the offer of a glass of champagne.

"You look great too, Evie." There was a trace of panic in Cormac's wide-eyed response. He'd obviously just realised that he'd broken one of the cardinal rules of gentlemanly behaviour. That of not fishing for compliments without first complimenting a lady's appearance.

He rang a finger around his collar. Swallowed.

Evie patted his arm. "Thanks, Cormac."

Cormac's shoulders lowered. The tension left his face.

"That's very sweet of you."

Was that a blush colouring Cormac's cheek? To Jake's amazement he had to concede that it was. It was hardly surprising. Evie had the power to make him forget what he was saying on an ordinary day, without trying. Dressed up and happy, she packed an even more powerful punch.

"What's on the agenda for tonight?"

Cormac directed his attention to Jake with a grateful look. "It's a major palaver."

"Cormac," Evie teased. "Don't be so cynical!"

Cormac grinned. "Well, it is. Once everyone has arrived and we've all had the chance to have a drink, the ceremony starts, in an area they've blocked off for now, behind the curtain."

A full-length white curtain divided the room.

"It's not a wedding ceremony, so I'm not best man. But I still have to step up with another ring." He tapped his jacket pocket.

"Oh, can I have a peek?" Evie asked.

Cormac shook his head. "I've been given very strict instructions. The ring is not to leave the pocket until I ask for it, Cormac, got it?" He did a fairly good impression of his brother. Accurate enough both Jake and Evie laughed.

"I can tell you it's an eternity ring. White gold, studded with diamonds all the way around."

Evie's eyebrows rose.

"He has good taste." Cormac grudgingly admitted. "She'll like it."

"She hasn't seen it yet?" Evie sounded surprised.

"She hasn't."

"Why would she?" Jake reached over and took his pint off the bar.

"I just thought...I thought Lisa might want to have some input into something she's going to wear for the rest of her life. I mean, what if she doesn't like it?"

Jake had never given a woman a ring. He'd never given much thought to the process. But now he was, it was a surprise to realise he did have an opinion about it.

When and if he gave a woman a ring, he would give her something that she would love. Because he'd know her and know what she liked.

He'd only known Evie a number of weeks, but her personal style was evident for anyone who took the time to pay attention. She wore stacked rings with gemstones on one hand, and nothing on the other. She liked gemstones and dull silver. And light, delicate pieces, rather than big, in your face, statement necklaces.

She wore a circlet of gold leaves on her head tonight, but that was out of character. Part of the cream and gold theme of tonight and not something she'd usually wear.

Today, she wore something he hadn't seen her wear before. A silver ring fashioned from a tiny silver coffee spoon, twisted around her finger.

He'd enjoy the process of choosing something for his perfect person. Something that would bring them joy, show how well he knew them, how in tune with their tastes he would be.

"After that, it's photographs in the garden, then dinner and dancing." Cormac caught someone's eye across the room. "I better—"

"Catch you later, mate."

Evie trailed a hand over Jake's sleeve. "There, that wasn't so bad, was it?" Her eyes twinkled. "Cormac seemed convinced."

"Cormac isn't our problem." He spotted Lisa heading across the room to them. "Here comes a real test."

He's killing me.

Pretending to be a couple shouldn't be this difficult. Evie put on a show every single day in work, pretending bonhomie and joking with Oscar, even when she didn't feel in the mood.

Even when one or both of them were hungover. Or on the umpteen occasions when the weather conspired against them, and the tour had to take place in torrential rain rather than blazing sunshine.

There wasn't a day when she couldn't play the part of a tour guide.

She was more than capable of playing the part of a smitten woman. The problem was *him*.

Jake Ridley was laying it on so thickly, she was smothered.

He refilled her glass regularly. Took every opportunity to hold her hand. To look into her eyes with such dedicated focus, she could almost believe he was as fascinated as he pretended to hear every word that fell from her lips.

He was making her feel strange. Giddy. An unwanted side effect was the spiking of her libido. Her head knew this was all pretend, but her body hadn't got the memo.

The meal was over, and the still happy couple were outside with their family having photographs taken in the garden. The band was setting up and Jake had just brought her another drink. This time orange juice at her request. Because there's only so much champagne anyone can drink before walking becomes a problem.

"I'm so glad you could both come."

A woman's hand landed on Evie's shoulder. She turned to see Cormac and Matt's mother standing next to the table. They'd been introduced briefly before the ceremony but hadn't had any chance to talk.

Evie said, "We're happy to be here." At the same moment as Jake waved at an empty chair at their table and said, "Won't you join us?"

He squeezed her knee.

Evie stopped herself from rolling her eyes. There was no need to put her on notice. She knew as well as he did that this would be a difficult test.

There was a stir across the room as Matt, Lisa, and the rest of the family walked in.

"The photographs are over then?"

"They are." Mrs Sweeney fixed her alert gaze on Evie. "Tell me about yourself, Evie. Are you from Dublin?"

"I'm originally from Kildare."

"Did you move up for work, then? I must admit, I was intrigued to hear from Matt that you drive one of those amphibious vehicles. That's amazing. Did you always want to drive for a living?"

Mrs Sweeney waved over a waitress who was circulating and seized a glass of wine off a tray.

"I didn't. I just sort of fell into it."

Jake was paying close attention. They'd briefed each other on the basics in order to best fake their relationship, but they hadn't covered each other's past in any details.

"How? How did you do that?" Mrs Sweeney wanted to know

everything. "It just seems so unusual. Did you go to college or..." She tilted her head to the side, like a curious bird.

Evie hated talking about her past. But there was no way to avoid these questions.

"I've always liked driving. But yes, I did go to college. I got a scholarship to study history. Unfortunately, my mother was sick, and I had to drop out."

She forced a tight smile.

Jake placed his hand over hers. She turned her hand over and interlaced their fingers. The support was just for show, but gave comfort all the same.

"I'm so sorry. Is she—"

"Evie's mother passed away." Jake found the words when Evie's throat tightened and closed.

"I didn't mean to bring up sad memories." Mrs Sweeney looked so distressed that Evie pushed past her discomfort to lighten the situation.

"I needed to be at home with her. And there weren't many jobs available that allowed me to do that. I upgraded my driving licence to be able to drive bigger vehicles and joined a local company who provided a school bus service."

Warmth filled her chest at the memory. If she hadn't had the chat with the children to look forward to every day, life would have been so much more unbearable. The hours meant she could spend as much time as possible with her mother and still make a living.

"I was lucky. Driving the school bus taught me that driving for a living was something I wasn't just good at, it was something I enjoyed. When I saw the advertisement for the job driving the Duck, I had to go for it."

"And you're a natural," Jake said.

The band started to play and the happy couple shimmied onto the dance floor up for their first dance to the cringeworthy 'Never Gonna Give You Up'.

"We should join them." Mrs Sweeney was on her feet, ready to dance. She scanned the throng, then spotted her target. "Cormac!"

Across the room, Cormac jumped. He looked to the exit but wasn't quick enough. Before he had a chance to move, his mother was on her way.

The dance floor was filled with gyrating bodies. There were all sorts of different variations of dances going on. A tall, thin man in his sixties was strutting around like Mick Jagger, pulling faces. His partner was wiggling her hips from side to side and pointing up and down to emphasise the song's lyrics.

There was a conga line weaving around the boundary. In short, it was complete mayhem.

"There's no way."

She enjoyed dancing, albeit badly. But she'd warned him before they came out for this evening that she wouldn't be dancing. Not in public.

"Maybe if they play a slow one?" Jake looked hopeful.

As though some heavenly body had heard his words, Rick Astley's anthem faded, and the music shifted to a slow number.

Three quarters of the dancers left the dance floor. Some repaired to the bar, and the others to their tables. A brave few couples melted into each other and swayed to the music.

"Come on." Jake jerked a head to the floor. "I know you said you don't dance, but that isn't dancing. Come sway with me."

Talking about her mother hadn't opened a wound, but it had put pressure on a scar, causing an ache.

"Okay." They walked out onto the dance floor.

Chapter Ten

Talking to Mrs Sweeney about her mother had brought the black days back. Those days weren't the ones where her mother had been at her sickest, but much earlier. The last months with her mother had been a time beyond coherent thought or planning. It had been as though she was on a roller coaster dropping through the air, falling, constantly falling. Hating every minute of it, but unable to escape. The only positives were golden moments they shared. They'd always been close, and her mother's illness brought them closer. Glittering golden moments of laughter or joy in the midst of pain were minutes to hold close.

The black days were the days before she left Dublin.

When she'd told Wyatt she had to drop out and move home.

She'd expected support. They'd moved in together at the beginning of their last year in university. They hadn't made any promises to each other, but they loved each other.

She was sure they'd loved each other. They'd both said it.

Wyatt had held her tight as she told him the news. He'd kissed her, then he'd eased back. "What about the rent?"

Had she heard him right?

"The—"

"I don't want to be crass, but what shall we do about the rent? I can't cover it all." His familiar mouth, the mouth she'd loved to kiss, curved in an apologetic smile.

"I can pay for next month, but I guess someone else will need to move in."

It was a one-bedroom flat. The only way he could move someone else in was if one of them slept on the sofa. Or the same bed.

Wyatt sat on the sofa. He hunched forward and looked at the floor. "That won't work. I'll have to move." He glanced up, latent anger flashing in the depths of his eyes. "I'm working on my thesis. I can't be homeless. Maybe you could—"

"Two months' rent."

"You're breaking the lease. They're renting to both of us."

"Your parents will have to help you out."

Evie had a full-time job all through college. She lived hand to mouth, barely scraping by. Her meagre savings were set aside for emergencies.

Pressure and pain threatened to overwhelm Evie.

The rent was important. She knew it was. But what about the other things Wyatt would be losing? What about losing her? And had he no sympathy for her situation? She had worked hard to gain her degree, and now it would have to be abandoned.

She could defer, but realistically, that dream was over.

Wyatt cared more about the loss of her half of the rent than he did about losing her.

"What do you expect from me?" Wyatt's bright blue eyes stared into hers. "You know I'm trying to ask my parents for as little as possible. Just because they can afford it, doesn't mean—"

She couldn't bear any more. "I'm sorry, Wyatt. I didn't plan any of this. I must give up my job as well as everything else. I'll put money into your account for the two month's rent tomorrow."

She stood and walked to the door. "I have to pack. Soo's brother Adam is driving me home tonight."

He hadn't helped.

He hadn't called when her mother died. She'd seen pictures on social media of his graduation. She'd heard through the grapevine that he'd moved to Germany for a Masters degree.

Talking to Mrs Sweeney had brought back that feeling. The cold, hard pain of having been a fool to believe that she might have had someone in her corner when things got difficult. That she and Wyatt might have been able to work together to support each other when things got tough.

Her father had run when he found out a child was on the way.

Any time she'd faced challenges through school, her mother had scooched down to her level and held her upper arms.

She'd muttered, "Don't let them know how much they've hurt you. Don't give them the satisfaction."

She couldn't count the times she'd squashed hurt down. Forced a bright smile and walked away. So instead of talking it through, instead of ranting and railing at Wyatt, and showing how much she needed him, she'd cut her losses.

Now, Jake's hand was in hers on the dance floor.

He swung her around so they were face to face.

"You're sad."

"A little. More melancholic."

He held their clasped hands up and snaked his other hand around her waist, pulling her close. "Let's dance."

She rested her head on his shoulder. Swayed.

She felt his laugh reverberated through his chest beneath her ear. His arm tightened. The painful feelings eased.

The music swelled. They started to dance. Jake's hand was flat against her back. She looked up, caught his eye. Connection zinged between them. A warm feeling filled her up, banishing the cold. She stroked the back of his neck.

Watched his eyes darken.

His head lowered; warm lips brushed hers. A featherlight caress and then they were gone. It was a feeling of I'm here. I understand you're sad, but I'm with you.

It was an illusion. She was just as alone as she'd ever been. This whole evening was about pretending. They both knew it.

But as his hand stroked her back, and their bodies moved as one, it was easy to pretend it was something more. To live the dream.

～

Evie stood on his foot. Jake didn't care. Every inch of her body was flush up against his. Body heat warmed her dress's soft silk beneath his hand. They were in a roomful of people, but his attention had narrowed to the woman in his arms.

He breathed in deep. Caught a trace of her spicy floral scent and felt his body tighten. Her touch on his nape filled him with electricity. He pressed his lips to her temple.

She tilted her face up, looking at him through her lashes.

They'd agreed to kiss to keep the illusion alive.

A light, pretend kiss wouldn't be enough. He wanted to kiss her for real. But not in a room full of people.

The room was filled with swaying couples. But something was happening near the doors to the garden. Cormac and a couple of wait staff were carrying high-backed chairs out onto the terrace.

Jake danced them closer.

Cormac spotted him when they were a few metres away.

"It's happening in twenty." He jerked his head towards the garden.

They'd spoken while Evie was momentarily distracted, and Cormac had leaked the surprise of the evening. A firework display that Lisa had organised without telling her husband.

"Let's go outside."

He grasped Evie's hand and dashed for the door. The fragrant garden was bathed in moonlight. There could be people out here, but if so, they were silent and hidden.

He'd checked out photos of this place on the website when pondering the wisdom of booking a room for the night. There had been a lake with picturesque benches and seats scattered through the garden. Cormac had said the fireworks would be over the water.

"There's a lake." He searched in the dim light and finally spotted the gleam of silvery water.

"And a seat." Evie pointed.

"Trying to get me alone, huh?" she teased. "You don't have to pretend to want to kiss me when there's no one around."

"Who says I'm pretending?"

"You're not pretending?" She walked to the bench. Looked back at him beneath her lashes. "You want to kiss me?"

She stopped. He almost crashed into her body in the moonlight.

The lake was a flat silvery disk. "It's beautiful." She turned to him again, and pushed his chest with a light touch, prompting him to sit on the teak bench.

She stepped between his legs.

"I want to kiss you, too. I've wanted to kiss you all evening."

He wanted to tumble her onto his lap. But this was her choice to make. Her game to play.

"A woman would have to be made of stone to resist slow dancing and moonlight." She looked at his mouth. "It doesn't have to mean anything."

She leant down and brought her lips to his.

Reason fled when her mouth parted and the kiss raged into flaming life. His hands were on her ribcage, her legs straddling his on the bench, and her core pressed against his hardening erection.

It means something.

The words flashed through his mind in silent answer to her statement. He didn't know what, but kissing Evie, really kissing

Evie, was not what he expected. He'd thought they could flirt, kiss, mess around.

Not that he would be in danger of getting naked and losing control at Matt and Lisa's wedding renewal.

A crack sounded across the water.

Evie jumped. Her head whipped around.

Jake shifted her off his lap, so she was sitting on the bench beside him. Her lipstick was smeared. He wiped the corner of her mouth with his thumb. "Watch."

Streaks of flying arrows lit up the sky. Followed by the sound of shots and exploding balls of brightly coloured light.

He looked away from the display. To Evie, whose mouth was open in wonder and delight. She clutched his hand tightly and didn't look away from the spectacle in the sky. He knew this for a fact.

Because he didn't look at anything except Evie.

Chapter Eleven

Evie'd seen fireworks.

And that was before the first rocket streaked into the sky. The fireworks had happened behind her closed lids when her mouth connected with Jake's on that bench. She'd been caught up in the feel of him. The illusion that they were one. She tried to damp down her desire as they pretended to be a couple, touching and kissing for appearances. But when Jake led her outside into the warm moonlight and they kissed for real, the spark set the fuse ablaze.

He'd held her as the display painted the sky every colour there was.

She hadn't thought about living here with him. Hadn't thought about all the things that could and may go wrong if they took their relationship from pretend to lovers. If the fates hadn't intervened, she would have been naked and in his arms, either out there in the moonlight or at home when the driver dropped them off.

She still couldn't work out if Cormac going rogue had been a curse or a blessing.

An abundance of whiskey and a sad song had seen Cormac

dissolve like a prawn cracker in the rain. He hadn't bailed. He'd wallowed. The previous maid of honour had brought her new husband as her plus one. Cormac found out she was married minutes after he started his serenade, when her husband thumped him.

Jake was holding her hand, looking at Evie as though she was special and precious, when Mrs Sweeney rushed out into the darkness in a panic. They hurried to her side.

"What is it?" Jake's voice was calm and steadying.

"It's Cormac."

Jake touched her arm. "Is he okay? Where is he?" "He's having a meltdown. Everyone here is friends with Matt and Lisa. Cormac isn't part of their social gang, and I can't find his cousin." She clenched and unclenched her fingers in agitation. "I don't want to spoil Matt's night." She'd wrung her hands together. "Please help."

"The car will be here in a moment." Jake had cupped her face in his hands. "You go home, I'll follow."

"We tried to get him upstairs, but he's singing again."

"I'll be there as soon as I can." He'd pressed a kiss to her lips. Not the sort of kiss she wanted, but the sort that was decent in front of someone's mother.

Matt's night hadn't been spoiled. But Evie's sure had. Jake called and said he wouldn't make it back before morning. By which stage, the blazing fireworks had been reduced to damp squibs. The moment had passed.

She joined Soo and Alex for brunch. Then returned to spend Sunday afternoon drilling the front of the house to replace vine eyes and wires to hold back the rambling rose which threatened to take the eye out of unwary delivery people.

This was turning into the weekend from hell. Jake had been wondering if it was too late to try to take a room in the hotel, rather than going back to his grandmother's house when Mrs Sweeney had raced outside calling for help.

One look in Evie's eyes has changed that. He didn't want to have breakfast with her and the entire Sweeney family, who were also staying at the hotel.

He wanted their first time to be special. Private.

Instead of spending the night with Evie, he'd spent it with Cormac. They'd talked long into the night. Cormac had opened up about his dreams for the future. He'd tried to persuade Jake that he and Matt should invest in a fledgling Indian restaurant start up, selling it with a gusto that was almost irresistible. At four in the morning, he'd confessed he hadn't had flu when Jake first arrived. That the real reason was because he didn't trust Global.

Jake had been forced to call Evie and tell her he wouldn't make it home.

He crashed on Cormac's sofa and left early the next morning before his host was up.

When he got home, Evie was out, and she wasn't answering her phone.

There was nothing he could do to repair his fractured love life, but he could check out some of the accusations Cormac had spouted the previous night. Jake tossed a couple of things in a bag and went to the office.

Early Monday morning, Jake placed a call to Christopher.

"You got my email?" He'd fired it off at seven. Christopher would have been up for an hour, had breakfast, and be dealing with the day's messages before starting in to work.

"I did." There was an edge to his boss's tone. "I think maybe you've forgotten who runs this company."

Jake's shoulders stiffened. "Clarify?"

"You know I welcome your suggestions, Jake. Your demands however..." He paused. Probably to take a deep drag of a cigarette. "I don't take well to anyone demanding anything."

Jake's email had been business-like and decisive. Not demanding or rude.

"This deal will fall through unless the Sweeneys feel supported and heard. The only way to do that is to give them written reassurances that we don't intend to strip their company for parts."

"You want me to put my name to an open-ended agreement. To make promises I can't guarantee to keep. I don't know what's happened to you, Jake." He didn't say it, he didn't need to. The incredulous tone in Christopher's voice indicated he thought his second in command had gone soft.

Jake took a deep breath. "Have you another solution?"

"Push it through. I need this company."

Jake rubbed the back of his neck. Shook his head as he stared down at his desk.

"We need to talk. I'll get on a plane."

"Don't bother. You've got a job to do. Get them to sign on the dotted line, or I'll send Pat to close the deal."

The line went dead.

Anger flashed like lightning.

He'd send Pat to close the deal?

The faint hunches he'd felt about Pat and Christopher colluding solidified into fact.

Christopher threw his weight around like a Roman Emperor. He even replied in meetings with a thumbs up or a thumbs down. Jake was good at his job. In the past couple of years, he'd closed more deals with less drama than anyone.

He didn't schmooze or get involved with company politics. He ran the numbers. Made sure that the financials worked, and the company Global was acquiring was a sound prospect. He trusted the company he worked for was honest.

He was a naïve idiot.

Pat and Christopher had met with the Sweeney brothers and neither of them had reported any of Matt's or Cormac's concerns.

And when Jake had contacted Pat to ask about their previous meeting, she'd played down any discontent.

Lying to Jake must be company policy.

He placed a call to his secretary. "Morning, Ellen."

"How's everything going, Jake? Sorry about being AWOL last week."

"Are the kids better?" Ellen was the mother of five primary school going kids. When one picked up something at school, it ricocheted through the family in a matter of days.

"Yes. Thank god. They're all back to school today."

"Glad to hear it." A sour taste was in Jake's mouth. Betrayal. Revealing everything to Ellen might be a risk, but he had to do it. He needed her help. "I think Christopher and Pat are working against me."

Silence stretched. "Can I speak plainly?" Ellen always kept the lines strictly drawn. He was the boss, and she was his secretary.

Jake didn't think of her like that. She was capable, efficient, and smart. They had different jobs, but she wasn't his inferior.

"I need you to."

"They're both shifty. Every time she steps into the lift, he dashes in after her. I've caught them plotting in the copy room a couple of times."

"I've never seen any of that."

"With respect, you're not often in the office. And you tend to see the best in everyone." She cleared her throat. "It's one of your most endearing qualities, actually."

I'm an idiot, but an endearing one. Great.

"I need you to pull some files and lock them in my top drawer." He read off a list of the recent acquisitions he and Pat had worked on. "These files are just for me, Ellen. I'm relying on your discretion on this."

"I understand."

She did. Ellen was unfailingly loyal. If his fears were founded,

Pat and Christopher may have left a trail. And if they had, he would find it.

"Are all the emails regarding acquisitions added to the files?"

"There can be hundreds, so just the crucial ones are printed out and added to the paper file. But as you know, we need to keep all the documents in case of any legal issues. I set up a system last year to file duplicates of them all in a locked area of the server."

Jake's eyebrows rose. "I don't remember that."

"Ah." Ellen sounded awkward. He imagined red flushing her face as it would if they were having this conversation face to face. "I took it upon myself. My workload was light—you were away and the final documentation for the acquisitions was being handled by Christopher's team. I remembered how difficult it was to extract all the relevant information regarding a client from the email system, and how long it took to do when we had limited time and resources and a crushing deadline."

"So you decided to go through my email discussions with our clients and make copies?"

"Yes, sir. I did." She never called him sir. Jake imagined her chin jutting. "I thought it was a good idea."

"It was. It was an inspired use of your time. Well done, Ellen." Something struck him. "And you did the same for the other partners?"

"Of course. The client file needs to be complete. Would you like me to put the emails onto a flash drive and lock that in your top drawer too?"

Chapter Twelve

On Monday, they met in the corridor upstairs. He in low-slung pyjama pants and nothing else. Her in an impulse buy from the Ann Summers evening (guaranteed to drive your partner wild!). He didn't even look up.

On Tuesday, she went into his room to get Cleo, and found him reading the Blue Aliens book in bed.

On Wednesday, he took them all out for dinner and acted like the perfect gentleman.

On Thursday, she stayed at Soo's because she didn't want to deal with him anymore.

Friday was John Woo Appreciation Society night. Evie was dressed in her Woo Hoo T-shirt, setting the bowls out for popcorn, and shoving bottles of beer into a bucket of ice when Jake strolled in.

"A real boyfriend would be a lot more attentive."

Jake had greeted her briefly in the kitchen when he came back from the office, then headed straight upstairs with his laptop under his arm and hadn't surfaced for hours.

Even now, as he fixed a cup of coffee, he hadn't changed out of his work clothes. And he looked distracted, just as he had all week.

"What?"

"You just seem remote. As if there's a problem. I guess we don't need to pretend to be in a relationship any longer." She should let it go. Damn it, she hadn't asked for this situation in the first place.

"I'm sorry. There are problems at work. I have to leave here early to catch the first flight to London tomorrow morning."

"Never mind. It doesn't matter. None of my business." She pushed off from the counter and started for the door. "The society arrives half an hour before the movie, so you should—"

A tanned arm snaked out and his hand clasped her upper arm.

Surprised, Evie stopped mid-stride.

Jake tugged, and all of a sudden, she was in his arms. His other hand slipped under her hair to cup the back of her head.

Without thinking, her body acting on complete impulse, Evie moved at the same moment he did, pulling him close as their mouths met in a blaze of heat.

There was nothing but the taste of his mouth. The touch of his hand against the side of her face. She couldn't get close enough, even though they were pressed together so close it would have been impossible to slip a piece of paper between their bodies. Her palms skimmed his shoulders. Gripped and released his bicep. She angled her head and pressed her temple against his body.

He stroked her chin. The side of her jawline. Traced the path his fingers had taken with his lips. Evie felt like she was melting. As though her bones had turned to liquid. She'd been kissed before. Hell, she'd had a couple of serious romances that might have developed into forever, if she had let them.

But no one kissed like he did.

With complete and dedicated focus. When she couldn't hold back a sigh, he stroked her back, making the hairs on the back of her neck stand to attention.

When she moaned, his hands spanned her ribcage, his thumbs teasing below her breasts.

Eleanore was in the other room, and they were in here making out like teenagers.

Evie placed both hands on his chest. A split second after she applied pressure, his lips left hers and his eyes opened.

"Your grandmother. We...I...we shouldn't." Somehow along the way, she'd lost the ability for coherent thought or communication.

Jake's hands fell to his side. "Of course. Of course, we shouldn't." He looked as stunned as she did. As though the moment had engulfed him by surprise, just as it had her.

She swallowed. Looked away from his hair, mussed by her eager fingers just moments ago. Tried not to think about his mouth. "I should go and get ready for this evening."

Before he could say anything to change her mind, Evie dashed from the room.

She sank onto her bed. Grabbed her pillow and hugged it to her stomach. This was a mistake. Kissing Jake Ridley had disaster written all over it. He'd ignored her all week. He wasn't interested in a relationship, and she wasn't either.

At least, she hadn't thought she was. But living so close to him was scrambling her senses, making her feel things that might not be real.

Cleo had taken to sleeping on his bed.

Cats made him sneeze.

He'd bought three lint rollers and handed them out like candy over dinner one night.

They all ate dinner together most nights. Jake and Eleanore had started talking about his mother in front of her. Alison seemed to infuriate them both equally, so much so that they'd even asked Evie's advice on how to deflect her constant meddling in Eleanore's affairs and attempts to infantilize her mother.

She hadn't had anything to do to get ready upstairs. She couldn't just stay there with Jake. She had to escape.

In the weeks he'd been in the house, she'd let down her guard.

She'd laughed at his jokes and felt her heart melt at the way he treated Eleanore. Cleo rubbed around his ankles in the kitchen every morning, and she was seconds away from wanting to do the same thing.

When she wanted something to drink, he reached for a glass for her from the top cupboard without being asked. They loaded the dishwasher in perfect harmony like a crack team competing for an Olympic sport.

He'd left his glasses on the table yesterday, and she'd dropped them off in his bedroom on the way to her own.

They were in a stealth pretend relationship.

She wanted a real one.

With a muttered curse, Evie got to her feet. She pulled her hair back into a ponytail and draped a scarf around her neck. If she could have got away with it, she would have put on sunglasses.

All ten members of the John Woo Appreciation Society were crammed into the living room, eager to enjoy this evening's offering—*Paycheck*. Jake had brought two chairs in from the kitchen for him and Evie and placed them opposite ends of the room. He needed distance tonight.

Needed some space to try to process what had happened earlier.

"Bless you, darling." Eleanore's friend Rita walked around him and planted herself on the chair he'd just carried in for himself. She waved across the room. "Cyril! Jake's brought in some hardbacked chairs! There's one over there." She pointed across to the other. "Such a relief." She said in a conspiratorial tone, even though her idea of a whisper was more a loud hiss. "Getting out of those sofas is impossible. And pulling Cyril out of one is frankly hazardous."

"I could—"

"You could bring me a beer? I'd love one."

Knowing when he was beaten, Jake did as he was asked.

Seniors prefer chairs they can get out of. A little-known fact that resulted in him and Evie squashed together in the 'grab you and don't let go' loveseat.

"The armchair upstairs is part of the same suite," Evie muttered under her breath as their knees bumped.

"Hmm." Jake rooted around in the cooler to his left and proffered a beer. Everyone was chatting, catching up with the week's events. They could talk privately without being overheard. "I didn't plan for this." He pointed to her and then back to himself. "You know."

"Are you referring to earlier?" Her tone was chilly. If there had been room to retreat, her voice indicated that she would.

"I mean this sofa. That you and I would be squashed on this sofa for the next hour."

She shot him a glare. "Closer to two." She looked disappointed in him. As though she expected more. She was the one who had pulled away in the kitchen earlier. She'd told him they shouldn't do this. But her body language and the things left unspoken signalled disappointment that he was doing exactly what she'd asked him to do.

Damn.

He leant closer to whisper in her ear. "I won't apologise for earlier. I wanted to kiss you and you wanted it, too. The only reason I don't want to sit next to you is it will be difficult to remain unaffected, being so close."

Her eyes opened wide, but she still stared straight ahead.

"I can feel your body heat across the space between us. I'm so damned aware of you, I think everyone can see how I feel."

She shot him a heated glance. He wasn't alone in this feeling.

"I know we shouldn't but—"

"Evie dear, could you get the lights?" Eleanore called from the other side of the room.

Evie struggled from the love seat's clammy embrace and walked away.

Jake sat in the dark as the movie started. He thought he knew what to expect from a John Woo film, but a young Ben Affleck deconstructing 3D tech showed he didn't have a clue. Evie hadn't come back from turning the light off. Not responding was the sane, sensible thing to do.

At least one of them was being sane and sensible.

Since the Sweeney party, he'd been a mess. He'd spent the week fighting a losing battle when it came to being attracted to Evie. He'd played cool when he passed her in the corridor wearing a flimsy red lace thing with laces up the front which barely reached the top of her thighs. He was plagued with daydreams, replaying the moment she'd straddled him on the bench, when he should be crunching numbers. Tonight, his control had finally shattered. Heat flared to flashpoint the moment his lips met hers, and before he knew it, he was pushing her up against the kitchen counter, wanting and needing more.

Of all the women in all the world, she was the one he couldn't have. There was still another week to go before she and Eleanore finalised the home share agreement. Three weeks living in the house with them both had put his fears to rest. She cared for Eleanore deeply, and the love was reciprocated. He couldn't imagine a better situation for his grandmother than to continue to live her life on her own terms with Evie's help.

He'd told his mother so.

He chewed his bottom lip as Ben Affleck flirted with a 3D projection of a pretty woman in a red dress.

If he and Evie started something and it didn't pan out, Eleanore would be distressed. A misstep could disrupt the home share relationship.

She thought it wasn't a good idea.

He knew it wasn't.

So why couldn't he stop thinking about her?

"Popcorn." Evie's shadowy form appeared from his left. She was bent over, trying not to block his view as she shuffled in front of him.

"I'll take it." He grabbed the bowl as she was swallowed up by the furniture. Then pushed the bowl closer so they had half the bowl on each of their knees.

"I didn't think you were coming back."

"I almost didn't." Her voice was low and the tone serious. "You've been so weird all week. You surprised me with what you said."

Unable to resist her pull, Jake reached for her hand in the darkness. "I'm surprised too. I haven't planned any of this. I don't know what I'm doing."

"Quiet in front!" Felix hissed.

Jake's lips curved upwards in a slow smile as Evie's fingers tightened around his.

Chapter Thirteen

"Thanks so much for taking me shopping, dear."

Evie and Eleanore were both pushing trolleys around the supermarket. Eleanore had explained that pushing one did double duty as both grocery basket and mobile walker.

Usually, Evie shopped and carried things home, but today they'd agreed to splash out on a taxi back to the house.

"Do you want a big one of these or—" Evie's hand hovered over the tequila shelf.

"The Patron Silver today, I think."

Evie put it into Eleanore's trolley. Along with the lime, salt, tortilla chips, and guacamole Eleanore had selected.

"Mexican night tonight, huh?"

Eleanore shrugged. "Poker night is tequila night. We finished the bottle last week, and I promised to restock."

They strolled around, picking things off shelves and tossing them into the trolleys.

"We need to have a little talk when we get home, Evie." Eleanore chose an elaborate cat toy of brightly coloured feathers suspended at the end of a bamboo pole. "It's important."

Evie's mind buzzed with unwelcome thoughts as they concluded their shop and went home. Perhaps Eleanore was having second thoughts about sharing her home with a near stranger. Maybe she regretted her offer and wanted to roll it back.

She could have seen Evie and Jake holding hands in the dark during the movie last night and have decided to say something.

Evie's jaw clenched as she put away the groceries.

In the weeks Evie had been living here, she'd really started to feel at home. More at home than she ever had living with Soo. Eleanore's home was full of friends. Friends who had totally embraced Evie's presence amongst them. Eleanore's house wasn't just a temporary place to lay her head. It felt like home.

She breathed in deep as she stacked Cleo's cat food into a bottom cupboard. It was home. For her and her cat. When she'd been looking for a new place from next door, there was anxiety about where she might find, but no regrets about moving on.

She'd lived there for a year. And lived here for mere weeks. But the thought of moving on made an ache bloom in her chest.

"Are you ready for our chat, dear?" Eleanore stood at the doorway, clutching a half-knitted something or other.

"Yes." She followed Eleanore into the sitting room and sat.

"This is rather awkward." Eleanore stared at the floor.

Evie's heart deep dived in her chest. She didn't want to make things difficult for her friend, but she also didn't think she could bear to be the one to suggest moving out.

She struggled to look unaffected and plastered on a gentle smile. "Just say what you're thinking. It'll be fine."

"Well, it's about tonight."

Tonight?

"I'll be out tonight."

"At poker night."

"Yes." Eleanore looked up and stared into Evie's eyes. There was a faint flush on her cheeks, as though she was steeling herself to say something she really didn't want to. "You and I are housemates. We see everything that goes on in each others' lives, and living so closely it's impossible to have secrets."

Oh, this did seem to be about Jake.

"I have certain arrangements that I don't wish my grandson and daughter to know about. Because it's none of their business, and I don't feel as though I must share. So, I have to ask if you will keep my affairs private. I will, of course grant you the same consideration."

The rush of relief was overwhelming. "Of course." Evie pressed a hand against her chest, feeling the pounding of her heart behind her hand. "I thought you wanted me to leave," she confessed in a quiet voice.

"Leave?" Eleanore frowned. "Why on earth would you think that, dear? As far as I'm concerned, you're more than a friend, you're family. I want to make our arrangement permanent."

Family. It had been a long, long time since she'd been included in anyone's family. "I want that too."

"I'll get the contract drawn up then. But back to these arrangements." Eleanore rolled her lips together and gripped her knitting. "I'll be out for poker night, but I won't be coming home until Sunday morning. Felix and I have decided to make a night of it."

"Oh." Evie tried not to look shocked. "Is this new?"

"Not exactly," Eleanore confided. "We've had an off and on arrangement for the past five years. If there's one thing I have to pass on to anyone, it's my mantra. Life is too short for what ifs. You'll never look back at your life and regret taking a chance on something good, but you will rue the day if you let fear hold you back.

"Felix and I are friends with occasional benefits, I suppose you'd call it. Anyway, he asked me to stay over. I said no, because I thought Jake would still be here, but as he's away—"

"I understand." Evie mimed zipping her lips and throwing away the key. "Our secret."

Jake's flight was delayed by two hours. The house on Bedford Street was dark and silent when he unlocked the front door and made his way inside. He strode into the kitchen and poured a glass of water.

The past few days had been a shit show.

As he'd feared, the emails had shown straight collusion between Pat and Christopher. They'd discussed potential problems without cc'ing him into the email threads. Had, on a couple of occasions, even discussed how they should proceed without informing him.

This was way more than keeping him in the dark. It was borderline fraudulent behaviour. He'd pushed contracts through without knowing the whole facts. Had assured targets that their employees' jobs would be safe, while at the same time Christopher and Pat were signing agreements to break those companies up and sell them for scrap.

He met Christopher and reiterated what he'd said on the phone. But he hadn't pushed his case. Or revealed the new knowledge he'd acquired.

Instead, he'd listened as the CEO dressed him down.

And afterwards, Jake had called his old friend, Suzette McDonald, and engaged her for her expert legal opinion.

The rest of the time had been spent downloading every single file and copying all the paperwork he needed to prove his case. He packed the papers into his briefcase with steely determination. It was sobering to realise he'd been oblivious to the undercurrents in his working environment.

That he'd blindly trusted that even though there had been some disgruntled clients, at the core Global Industries was an ethical company. Whatever the future, he couldn't let the Sweeney brothers go through with this deal. Because Christopher's refusal to put anything in writing wasn't because he couldn't guarantee that Global wouldn't change things at Sweeney Brothers. It was because doing so would go against his plans.

Jake hadn't found the paperwork confirming his suspicions yet. But he would. Last night, after meeting Christopher, he'd intruded into his assistant's private time, and driven out to her house.

They'd sat in her back garden, watching the kids play and splash in a paddling pool while he'd opened up and told her what he suspected was going on, and what he intended to do about the situation.

Her husband stacked the dishwasher and filled the coffee machine as Ellen listened intently to everything he had to say.

"I knew there was something wrong." She twisted her hands together. "I'm so glad you're trusting me with this."

"You've always been loyal and straight with me, Ellen. I appreciate that." One of her boys kicked a football that bounced off Jake's leg. He tossed it back. "What happens next isn't going to be pretty. There will be a lot of flak flying around, and we'll have to dodge it as best we can."

He stared into her eyes.

"At the end of this, there won't be a Global Industries. I will have taken it down. But I want you to come with me, and we'll build something new. Something better. Something where the little guy doesn't get steamrolled in the pursuit of money."

The corners of her mouth turned upward, gradually building to a wide, happy smile. "I'm with you one hundred per cent. Tell me what I need to do."

There was a faint sound, a television perhaps. Jake trudged upstairs. There was a thin line of light visible underneath the door of Evie's sitting room. She was still awake.

He stood still for a long moment. Contemplating. The urge to knock burned bright. He wanted to wrap his arms around her. To bury his face in her soft hair and confide everything.

He'd spent his whole working life acting as a lone wolf. Ruthlessly focused on completing tasks and climbing the ladder. It stung to accept that his mother's ambition for him to be a success, to be the best, had influenced him, but it had.

His father worked long hours. Jake and one of his brothers had followed suit, and his youngest brother had escaped to teach English as a foreign language in Marbella. Effectively putting himself out of their mother's influence.

Somehow, along the way, the work had become everything.

Talking to Ellen today had brought one thing into clear focus. It wasn't too late. Now he was aware of the facts, everything had changed. He could be a better man, focused not just on money, but also on people. His loyal secretary had placed her faith in him, and he wouldn't disappoint.

The memory of Evie's hand in his made him curl his fingers into his palm. In the plane, he'd stared out unseeingly at the clouds, imagining her face. On Friday night when he'd taken her hand, she had tried hard not to react and alert the others. Her thumb stroked over his knuckles in a soft caress that heated his blood. She hadn't turned to look at him, but kept her gaze glued to the movie. But the slow, intimate smile that curved her lips was not for on-screen Affleck, it was for him.

Remembering that smile, Jake wanted to kiss her so bad, he ached.

The situation with Global was about to blow up. He couldn't jeopardise the outcome by confiding in Evie now.

With a soft sigh of disappointment, Jake kept walking.

Chapter Fourteen

I f there was a book of men, Evie hadn't read it all the way through. She couldn't count the times the guys at work had confessed to not understanding their wives or girlfriends. And she'd never chimed in with her own problems deciphering the workings of the male mind.

All she knew was that Jake had been tightlipped about his reasons for returning to England and had been decidedly different since his return.

On Friday, they'd been kissing in the kitchen and holding hands through a John Woo film. She thought she knew what that meant. That they were both feeling attracted. Despite the difficulties inherent in taking it further.

She'd thought about him all weekend.

On Monday night, she heard the front door open and had waited with bated breath for a rap on the door. She'd somehow persuaded herself that he might want to see her as much as she needed to see him.

She'd flicked ahead a few pages in the book of men and lost her place. The clues from the week before didn't make sense. In her previous relationships, she'd closed the book before coming to the black moment. Had shoved the book of men in a drawer, rather than battle through.

This time, she didn't even have the luxury of giving up on the book of men. From being everywhere in their shared space, Jake was the invisible man.

He showered, ate breakfast, and was gone before she climbed out of bed in the morning. He came home for lunch with Eleanore and made an excuse to skip eating with them in the evening. Except for the night she was out with Soo.

If she were the type of person who suffered from paranoia, she'd be a wreck, wondering what she'd done wrong to make him avoid her again. Instead, she stiffened her shoulders and put it down to once again a misreading of the book of men.

So, when she twisted her key in the lock on Wednesday evening, Evie had no expectation of seeing Jake.

Not least sitting on Eleanore's eighteenth-century slipper chair with the half height legs and a gaggle of women staring at him as though he were either a saviour or a god.

"Hi, dear! Have a good day?"

At Eleanore's greeting, Evie glanced away from the disturbing tableau and swerved into the kitchen.

Eleanore was cutting cheese into chunks.

"Can I help you with anything?"

"Yes, please." Eleanore's eyes were suspiciously sparkly. "The girls and I were having some sherry, and I thought maybe I should do cheese and grapes on sticks to help keep us on track."

"Which girls are these?" Evie tried to remember which of Eleanore's groups were taking over the place tonight.

"Tonight is knitting group, the Knit Nuts, dear. I'm the teacher."

Evie remembered. She'd managed to avoid the knitting group's meetings so far, but they'd chatted about the Knit Nuts over the dinner table and the projects those attending were working on. Eleanore's mouth had turned down at the corners when Evie'd had to confess to not having ever knitted or crocheted anything in her life.

Peals of laughter floated down the hallway.

Evie got a platter from the cupboard and started to thread cheese and grapes onto cocktail sticks. "I didn't realise you had such a large class."

Eleanore pursed her lips, puffed out a sigh, and opened the fridge to take out another block of cheddar. "Normally, I have five or six students. Unfortunately, I made the mistake of telling someone at the WI meeting that my grandson would be helping this evening, so fifteen have turned up."

Jake? Helping? How?

"Jake's helping?"

"He's a master at Aran stitching. You should see the fisherman's jersey he made for his twentieth birthday." Pride shone in her eyes.

"He knits?" Evie was pretty sure she'd never seen a chapter with that heading in the book of men.

"He knits brilliantly." She smiled, as if remembering. "Didn't you see the picture in the hallway? Go look." She waved out the door. "On the left, over the half-moon table."

Evie snuck out to examine the framed photographs she walked past every morning and every night. Blurry snapshots of family. She peered close. In one, a little boy wearing shorts beamed at the photographer in pure joy. He held up his work in progress. A long panel of blue knitting fed onto two bright-pink plastic knitting needles.

Evie's heart melted.

Knit one, purl one, is how Evie had imagined knitting class would go. Instead, it was a gossipy get together with yarn and needles. Eleanore sat at pride of place in her favourite chair. The chair next to her was kept vacant, for knitters in peril, who dropped in one at a time holding their knitting up for her advice and perusal.

Sometimes she demonstrated a complicated stitch as they looked on with total concentration. Other times she took pity on the desperate and knitted on for a few lines to help them out.

Jake employed a different method. He was more of a travelling guru. People needing his help held up a hand and called him to their sides.

He talked knitting. Had heated discussions about maintaining tension. And generally charmed the pants off them.

"If you're in the class, you need to be working on a project," Rita said from Evie's right. She gestured at the basket of brightly coloured balls of wool in the centre of the table. "At the end of every project, we donate leftover wool to the basket. Just choose something from there. There are extra needles in Eleanore's fishing box under the table."

"I can't knit."

Rita snorted. "Everyone can knit."

If there had been anyone with the skill in Evie's life growing up, she would have loved to have learned at their knee—as Jake had. But there hadn't. No grandparents. No father. And a mother who worked all the time. Maybe she'd known how to knit, but Evie didn't think so.

"Not me." She forced a tight smile.

"Jake!" Rita waved across the room. "Code red! We've got a knitting virgin over here who needs your help, stat!"

He sauntered over. Squatted down on his haunches next to her chair, bringing his face level with hers. "Is it true?"

"My virginity? Unfortunately, so." Jeez, she was flirting. And flirting badly. When any self-respecting virgin should ignore him after his hot and cold flimflam.

Rita and the woman sitting next to her started a conversation about someone they both knew who seemed to be having a torrid affair.

Jake smiled. "I can help you with that."

She pressed her lips together to stop any more stupid bad flirting from taking over.

"Let's get you some needles and yarn, and I'll give you the basics."

He opened the fishing box and peered inside.

On impulse, she asked, "Are there any pink needles?"

He rooted around, then held a pair aloft. The same pair pictured in the photograph in the hallway. "There's a story behind these." He rubbed the beads at the non-pointed end with his thumb. "I'll tell you sometime."

Jake spent a productive hour on Zoom with Suzette reviewing the files. They found plenty of evidence that Global's UK operation was dirty to the core.

But in the days since he discovered the truth, a bigger truth had become evident. It wasn't enough to protect Sweeney Brothers. He needed to reform Global from the inside out.

There were companies who were prepared to downsize, to completely restructure their workforces, in order to become profitable and grow within the Global family.

Jake had no problem with that. Being profitable should be every company's bottom line. And they needed to understand that sometimes it wasn't possible to achieve without some pain.

Where Global sinned was in the fact they lied. They sold the idea of some other magic bullet they could use to transform their firms. They'd persuaded owners of those companies to sign on the dotted line, then done whatever they wanted, anyway.

Global's management needed to be held to a higher code of accountability. They couldn't just promise one thing and do another.

Suzette had confirmed what he suspected. That Christopher and Pat must have made the decision to hide facts from Jake because they knew his moral code wouldn't accept their behaviour. In the latest emails Ellen had copied from the server, Christopher had briefed Pat on their recent meeting.

Under no circumstances do we comply with his demands, he'd written arrogantly. *I've told Jake that we can't give written assurances and he backed down, so I think he's neutralised. He said, she said, hold no legal weight but once something is committed to paper, it exists forever. As usual, make sure to delete this.*

Christopher was not tech savvy. Neither was Pat. They'd added 'delete this' to the end of every email they considered private. And had no doubt deleted them from their local devices and felt completely confident their tracks had been hidden.

But the back-ups on the server remained.

Christopher was right. Once you commit something to writing, it does live forever.

Jake had felt sick reading through. He'd trusted Pat and thought he had her respect. But the way she instantly and completely agreed with everything Christopher said revealed her total duplicity. He'd been managed. Steered by invisible hands. Used as a frontman to bestow legitimacy to a fraudulent team without honour.

It wasn't about this one job any longer.

He needed to get more evidence. He needed to bring them down.

There was a high-pitched noise from downstairs. He terminated the call. Walked to the top of the stairs and listened.

"Jake!" His grandmother's voice, calling.

He dashed down the stairs. Rounded the curve in the return to see her standing at the foot with a tea towel slung over her shoulder.

He slowed his momentum and skidded to a stop six inches from her. "I thought you were in trouble."

She made her *don't be ridiculous* face: a combination of squinty eyes and twisted mouth.

"If by *trouble* you mean about to have breakfast and wondering if my favourite grandson would like to join me, then yes, I guess you could say I'm in trouble."

"I'm your favourite?"

She smiled. "Don't tell your brothers. I'll deny it."

"Full Irish?"

Eleanore spent hours every day trying to fatten him up. He walked over to the stove and examined the contents of the frying pan. Bacon, sausages, hash browns, tomato, black and white pudding.

Beans and eggs in their own saucepans on the side.

She must have been cooking for ages. Two faded blue and white plates were on the table, and the teapot had a knitted cosy wrapped around it, and two cups ready.

"Of course. This looks fantastic."

She handed him a plate and waved at the feast. "Help yourself. I'll pour tea." She lifted the pot and poured. "I can't believe I've had you under my roof for almost a month and not made you breakfast yet. You're always dashing out the door before I'm even up. And then when you are here at the weekends, you've had your cinnamon roll before I've had time to get the frying pan out."

He placed the plate down on the table and picked up the empty plate.

"What'll you have?"

She told him.

They sat opposite each other. She patted the newspaper she'd placed next to his plate. "The paper's there. I've already read it."

"I'll read it later." He spent so little time with Eleanore, there wasn't any way he would dilute the time they had together by reading the paper.

"How much longer do you think you'll be on this job?" Her expression was keen and interested.

Long enough to explode my life.

"I'm not sure. Probably another couple of weeks."

"And then it'll be back to London?"

A melancholy ache filled him. "I suppose it will be." But really, what did he have to go back to? For the past five years, he'd dedicated his entire time to his job, and now that job would be no more. His focus on work had weakened his friendships, as he was often away.

Eleanore tilted her head to the side. "You don't really want to go back, do you?"

Jake wasn't about to lie to the one woman who'd always been there for him since he was born. "Not really."

"You don't need to, you know. The whole top floor is free. You can have a home share agreement too."

He felt more at home here than he ever had anywhere his entire life. He liked being able to have meals with his grandmother. To battle the cat for the privilege of sitting on his office chair.

"You have a crush on Evie." It wasn't said as a question, but rather a statement of fact. Eleanore swiped a piece of toast around her plate.

"I—"

She held up a hand. Not wanting to hear his denial.

"Now, no need to say anything more about it." She rolled her lips together. Tilted her chin down and looked at him through her fringe like Lady Di. "Except I'm pretty sure she feels the same."

Chapter Fifteen

"Your friend is on the tour today, isn't he?" Oscar scanned the tickets for a family of three with the scanner on his phone and waved them up the Duck's metal stairs. "This is the guy who spilt coffee all over himself, right?"

Ever since Evie'd confessed that she now lived in the same house as 'shirt guy', Oscar and the other guides had been fascinated. The team spent much time hanging around before and after tours, and the usual way of passing that time was to gossip.

Evie knew so much about Oscar's relationship with his wife she hadn't been able to look her in the eye at the Christmas party.

And the exploits of the unattached tour guides were always dissected after each weekend. If they had stories they wanted to share. And they did. The guys were frank and funny, and on occasion, downright hilarious.

Evie usually took the role of an amused bystander.

But living with 'shirt guy' catapulted her from audience to main event. She wasn't used to being the centre of attention. Still, after years of listening rather than confessing, she had no option.

"He's bringing some clients."

Cold dread settled in her stomach. Oh. She'd forgotten. She and Jake were supposed to be in a relationship. And Oscar was a bloodhound when it came to relationships.

He worked out who was flirting with who in the Duck with the faintest of clues. He had legendary gaydar. He could spot a potential proposer and have a carpet tile out of his box of tricks under the front seat and on the ground for a bended knee before they had the ring out of their back pocket.

He would know she and Jake were faking.

She swallowed.

Today, they would have to pretend to be a couple. In full view of the love whisperer.

"Anything going on between you and him?" Oscar shot her a glance.

Heat flushed Evie's face. "Well, um—"

Oscar punched the air. "I knew it!" He grinned. "He's kissed you, hasn't he?"

If a sinkhole suddenly appeared on the side of St Stephen's Green, she'd run and jump into it to escape Oscar's triumphant crowing.

She breathed in deeply. "He has."

"Boyfriend and girlfriend?"

"Well, we're taking it slow." She should be talking their relationship up rather than minimising it, but with Oscar's finely honed instincts it was better to be vague.

"I knew it." Oscar shoved his phone into his pocket. "I won big today."

A tall figure dressed in jeans and army surplus jacket walking down the other side of the street with a guitar case strapped to his back waved and crossed the road.

"Evie! It's true then. You're back and driving this brute."

Evie walked her mother's old friend Finn away from the Duck and back to the railings. "I haven't seen you in an age." The moment the words left her mouth she remembered exactly when and where she'd last seen him. Playing music at her mother's wake.

He must remember too, because a shadow passed over Finn's face. "It's been far too long. We're playing Dublin at Christmas. Give me your number, I'll put your name down at the door." She handed him her phone. "Maybe you might even play in your mother's memory?" Evie's mother used to perform with Finn's band every Christmas.

"I'm not of her standard. You know that."

Oscar waved to get her attention.

"I have to go."

Finn pulled her into a bearhug. "Just one song. Think about it."

Finn crossed the road and disappeared into the crowd.

Evie rejoined Oscar just in time to see Jake come into view.

There must have been an important meeting, because Jake wore his navy Tom Ford with narrow pinstripe. Her mouth had gone dry the last time she'd seen him in it, so she'd sneaked a peek at the label inside the jacket when he'd left it draped over the chair in the kitchen.

She liked looking at him no matter what he wore. And hadn't thought she had a boss fantasy. But something about the way the combination of sharp suit, snow-white shirt, and a tie made her want to wander over and perch on his knee with a shorthand notebook.

There was no trace of his usual stubble.

Photographers spent hours with hair putty on male models to achieve the springy wave that swept across his forehead.

He walked abreast with Lisa, who looked left and right, busy checking out her surroundings.

Behind them, Matt and Cormac were deep in conversation.

Jake's gaze didn't waver. All his attention was firmly focused on her. It was the hottest thing she'd ever seen.

And it was obviously doing the trick because there was a clearing of a male throat to her right. "Fair play," Oscar whispered. He held his palm up. "Don't leave me hanging."

She completed the high five.

When she looked back, the little party was approaching. They'd cut it fine; the rest of the guests were already onboard.

"Good morning!" Oscar's voice rose in tour guide mode.

"Good morning." Jake stepped close. He tilted Evie's face up to his and lowered his lips to hers in a kiss. If she'd been a casual observer, she'd have swooned and gone all mushy at the sight of obvious true love.

As one half of the embrace—one half who knew they were only pretending—she damn near fell over as a wave of passion flooded her and made her knees weak.

She grasped his arms as he continued to kiss way longer and more thoroughly than was decent. When she finally came up for air, it was to see a huge grin on Oscar's face.

"Our lovely driver, Evie, everyone."

The entire busload had been watching.

"Give her and her fella a big roar!"

Jake kissed her cheek quickly. "See you later, babe."

Her passengers' roar in her ears, Evie made her way behind the wheel and set off on her usual route around the city.

As they were the last to board, Jake and the others were at the back of the Duck. To Evie's relief, Oscar had no time to make more than the passing comment or tease, as there was just too much necessary commentary he had to make.

When they finally were on the final stretch back to where the tour started, Oscar sat down in the passenger seat. "He's lovely, your fella. I approve."

She raised an eyebrow.

"He's a great roar, too."

She shot him a look. One that spoke volumes.

"I didn't say anything." Oscar smirked. "He does though. It's not every day we get a guy in a suit wearing the helmet."

She indicated and changed lanes. "His clients seemed to enjoy themselves?"

"Oh, they did. Like a bunch of big kids. Just the way it should be." He stood and faced his audience again.

Then he looked back. "Park up and go for lunch with Jake. I'll deal with the paperwork and lock everything up."

"I can—"

Oscar leant in. "Believe me, you want to spend some time together. He's been staring holes in the back of your head."

When Evie jumped down from the Duck, Jake was right there, waiting. She greeted him with a kiss. A brief brush of her lips against his—nothing that would cause anyone to roar, but enough.

Enough to persuade a stranger they were in love.

It should look convincing because they both knew there was nothing fake about this fake relationship. Neither of them was pretending.

They chatted with the Sweeneys for a while. Then Jake checked his watch. "I'm taking the afternoon off, guys. I'm taking Evie to lunch."

"You are?"

"You don't have another tour today, do you?"

"No, one of the other driver's asked to switch shifts—" The truth dawned. "You didn't."

He grinned.

"You did! Who knew about this? Does Oscar know?"

"I just asked him if there was any way he could swing you the afternoon off. And he did. Come on. We have a reservation."

There were plenty of good restaurants in the centre of Dublin. When they turned down Dawson Street, Evie would have bet money on Café en Seine being their destination, but Jake just kept walking.

He took a right. Then very quickly, turned left. Down an alley, a few more twists and turns then he rapped on a red painted door.

"Is this a restaurant?" She searched the front of the building, but there was nothing to indicate this was anything but a personal dwelling.

"It is today."

An Indian woman dressed in a sari welcomed them in. Jake introduced her as Veda.

She relieved Evie of her jacket and hung it on a coat stand just inside the front door. It was the only garment hanging there.

The walls were pained a dull saffron gold. Distemper, rather than emulsion. An ornate pierced lamp fitting threw firefly shadows onto the ceiling.

Threadbare Persian rugs older than Eleanore covered tongue-and-groove floorboards.

Jake held her hand as they followed Veda through the house to a room at the end.

"What is this place?" she whispered.

"You'll see."

Veda waved them into a room set up with a dining table covered in a pristine white linen tablecloth. A glass vase filled with white orchid flowers sat in the middle. Two places were laid opposite each other.

"Sit, sit, Jake. And welcome. I'll bring you the wine, yes?"

"Thank you, Veda."

Then they were alone.

"Okay, you've surprised me. I thought I knew everywhere, but this...how on earth did you find it?" She looked around. "Is this even a restaurant?

"Veda is a master chef. Cormac is investing some money to help her open her own restaurant. When I confided I wanted to take you somewhere new, he asked Veda to make us a home-cooked meal. He's trying to persuade both me and Matt to join him in the investment."

"Veda's making us lunch in her house?" Evie couldn't believe it. When Jake first arrived in the country, he had been such an isolated workaholic he hadn't even visited Eleanore for a week.

Now he was talking about investing in a restaurant with people he'd met mere weeks ago, and able to organise a true surprise at a moments' notice with the help of his friend.

"Your friendship with Cormac is going strong, then." She couldn't help but feel a twinge of some nasty, mean-spirited emotion when she thought of going alone after that party, while Jake spent the night with Cormac.

Before Jake could answer, Veda walked in carrying a chilled bottle of Mateus Rose.

"Veda. Jake has just told me we're in your house and you're making a meal for us. I'm blown away. Thank you so much for making such a special experience for us."

Veda poured a thin stream of pink wine into their glasses.

"You're welcome." She patted a thick white linen napkin around the bottle's neck, drying an errant drip. "I'm delighted to present my signature dish for you today, I call it sunset stars. I'll be back in a while."

Veda left them alone.

"I can't believe we're having a private tasting in a chef's home. She must be very keen to secure investment."

Jake traced his fingertip over the back of Evie's hand, which rested on the table. She turned it over and he stroked her palm. "She is. But I don't want you to think I'm taking advantage of the situation—she negotiated a very healthy fee before agreeing."

"I should hope so." Evie tried to keep track of their conversation, but the touch of his skin on hers was causing her to lose focus. His thumb flattened against the faint blue threads of her veins in her wrist. Perhaps he could feel the high-speed flutter of her pulse.

He looked at her mouth.

"What are we doing?" Her words were no louder than a whisper. The question was one of the most important she had ever spoken. Evie knew what she wanted to do. She wanted to throw caution to the wind and recklessly surrender to the emotion and impulses crowding her senses. But he was a different story. He was hot and then cold, like the Katy Perry song.

"Eleanore thinks I have a crush on you." Jake lifted her hand and pressed his mouth against her palm.

Evie shivered. "Yes, she told me."

She wanted to ask if it were true. But asking the question shoved the door open for rejection. For him to retreat and avoid her as he had for the past few days. She'd never been able to do casual. And what she felt for Jake was already dangerous. What if she ...

He still held her hand captive, his fingers lightly encircling her wrist. She flexed her fingers and stroked the side of his face.

He looked up. The moment their gazes connected, the futility of running pros and cons in her mind became clear. They could say whatever they wanted about how letting this attraction between them bloom to life was a bad idea. But being in control of what was happening between them was an illusion.

His eyes blazed azure, desire evident in their depths.

The sound of heels heralded the approach of their private chef, bringing them no doubt a meal to die for. But the spell between them glimmered in the air weaving silken threads of attraction between their two bodies, urging them closer.

The door opened.

Jake released her hand and leant back, a sensual smile playing over his lips.

The future was crystal clear, sparkling with possibilities. If she was brave enough to reach for it.

Life's too short for what ifs.

Chapter Sixteen

Veda thought they were in love. She didn't say anything, but it was evident in the sneaked glances and tiny smiles she shared while serving them when Evie wasn't looking. He felt no need to explain they were just friends. Because he didn't have any friends he wanted to kiss senseless. His motivation for bringing her somewhere she'd never been before was to surprise. Not to seduce.

Surprise it had. And more than that, delight.

In a roomful of people, Evie took a back seat and people watched. She always wanted to know about Eleanore's day when she returned home, and generally didn't volunteer information about her own. She was at ease in company, but shy. Reticent. When he'd kissed her before the plastic helmet wearing passengers in the Duck, she'd been self-conscious and disconcerted.

There were plenty of other places he could have taken her for lunch. Places where they would be surrounded by strangers. This was much better.

She delighted in every mouthful of Veda's wonderful dish. Begged to learn the secret ingredients so earnestly that Veda was charmed into almost revealing them.

With nothing to distract—he was captivated by every expression that played out on her expressive face. She waved her hands around as she told stories. Her eyebrows rose and lowered, and her tone shifted to alto as she unconsciously imitated Oscar while recounting a previous tour incident.

She was so enchanting; he could watch her all day.

He may have not had seduction on his mind, making this lunch date. But attraction permeated the air like the scent of jasmine on a summer's night. It was beginning to feel as though there was nothing in the world more important than their being alone together.

After Veda closed the door on them, they stood on her doorstep looking out at the world. Even though he had emails to read, strategy to plan, right now Jake just let life be. She stood beside him. There was no need for words. No need to try to explain anything. To make plans. It was as though they had dropped into a slow-moving river, and were surrounded in its warmth as they floated downstream.

Evie's hand slipped into his.

He looked into her eyes.

The corners of her lips tilted up in that smile that made his heart stutter. "Let's go sit under a tree in Stephen's Green and make out."

He checked his watch.

She huffed. Pulled her hand from his and crossed her arms.

"Forget it, it's fine." She shook her head from side to side as if shaking herself out of a fever dream.

"What happened?" He touched her shoulder, prompting her to look at him.

"I misread the situation. Let's just forget it. You're busy. I get it."

Ah, checking the watch.

"It's three o'clock. Cinema Girls are going to the three o'clock show." He reached for her hand. "Which means if we hurry, we can have at least two hours alone before Eleanore's home."

Her eyes widened. "Let's go."

∾

This was all going down like a country song. Neither of them had brought a car into work, so they raced through Dublin so fast you might have thought their house was on fire. Jake held her hand and wove through crowds of people on the pavements like a slalom skier.

She tugged on his hand. "Wait."

He turned, a question in his eyes, as if considering she was changing her mind. As though at least one of them had snapped back to cold, hard reality.

She jerked her head to the side, indicating a shop she wanted to enter. "Wait here."

He released her hand and backed up against the glass window. She darted around, grabbing a box of condoms and a tube of lube.

"You need a bag?" the chemist asked.

"I need a bag." She shoved the white paper bag into her handbag and claimed Jake's hand again. He closed the distance between them and kissed her hard. If there had been any reservations about taking this step, about breaking her six or was it seven-month celibate spell, they were dissolved like instant coffee grains in boiling water.

She was in a moment. A precious moment. A moment for now, not for tomorrow or next week.

He started walking again. She hurried to catch up. To walk by his side back to the home they shared.

His hand rested on the back of her neck as she unlocked the front door.

"Check she's still out," she whispered against his mouth as the door closed behind them. "Meet you upstairs."

He strode through the downstairs rooms as Evie rushed up to her bedroom and hurriedly made the bed. There was a pile of laundry on a chair, so she opened the wardrobe and hurled the clothes inside, out of sight.

What should she do? Lie on the bed?

Nerves rattled around inside.

Then he was at the doorway. And everything changed.

"She's out." He walked to her, but she met him halfway. Time seemed to still as his hands cupped her cheeks and he held her head in exactly the perfect position for their kiss. When they finally broke apart, both were breathing fast.

"I love this suit." She slipped his jacket off and it slid to the floor. "You look very sexy in a tie." She inexpertly unfastened it. He didn't try to help, just stood with passion burning in the depths of his eyes.

She sucked in her bottom lip and concentrated on opening every button of his shirt before tugging it from his trousers and shoving it off his shoulders.

The moment the white cotton hit the ground; he came to life.

"Your turn." She had undressed him slowly because she wasn't very good at it. He undressed her slowly because he was very good at doing so. By the time she stood in her black lace bra and matching knickers, her heart was beating out of control.

"You're beautiful." His fingers caressed her shoulders, stroked across her collarbone.

He took her hands and placed them on his chest. "Touch me."

It was only when he held her so tenderly, kissed her cheekbone, and smiled against her mouth that Evie realised she might be in trouble. She might really be in trouble. He literally swept her off her feet and carried her to bed.

"I've always fantasised about that," she murmured as she stroked down his perfect six-pack.

"About my abs?"

Honestly, the guy was incorrigible. The thought of what Jake looked like without his clothes and what his abs might feel like had snuck into a few of her fantasies, but she wasn't about to admit that right this moment.

"About someone picking me up and carrying me to bed."

"No one's ever tried?"

He smiled when she shook her head no.

"In that case, it shall be our thing. I'll carry you everywhere."

Her laugh came out as a snort. "That might be a dead giveaway to your grandmother that we're sleeping together."

His eyes darkened. He unfastened her bra and slipped the straps from her shoulders. "Do you—"

She reached over the side of the bed for her handbag. Pulled the white paper bag free and tossed it over.

He placed the lube carefully on the bedside table. Took a small silver packet from the box and placed it on the bed next to her hip.

She'd never wanted someone this much. Had never had someone explore her body with such dedicated focus. She tried to unfasten his trousers, but he told her no.

He wanted to touch her.

To taste her. To make her happy.

Then Jake eased the strip of lace from her body and settled between her legs.

Chapter Seventeen

"We should move." Evie sounded sleepy. Her head was nestled against his shoulder, and one leg was thrown over his.

Jake stroked her elbow. "Yes, we should."

Evie snuggled closer. "We can't let Eleanore find us in bed together."

"We definitely can't." Jake tilted her mouth up to his and traced her full bottom lip with his fingertip. Then followed the path his finger had taken with his mouth. "Two hours isn't enough." They'd had sex twice, and he was ready to go again. She curled up sexy and boneless. His body was tight and tense. All he could think about was sliding her on top and sinking into her heat.

But the Cinema Girls would be arriving for their post movie early dinner and chat just as they did every week. And he couldn't be caught like this.

"I have to get up."

Her hand traced his erection, plainly visible beneath the sheet. "You are up." Her wide smile. He wanted to kiss it right off her mouth. To make her feel as desperate and aroused as he was.

"We better shower." He picked her hand off him and swung his legs out of bed. "Do you want to go first?"

"Okay." She held the sheet up over her beautiful breasts. Was there a trace of hurt in her eyes? He walked around the bed and sat down next to her. "You know if we were guaranteed to be alone, I'd stay in bed with you and fuck all night, don't you? I don't ever want to let you go."

The words took him by surprise. Not the sex all night part—that was a no-brainer. But the not ever wanting to let her go.

Because he would let her go. The best this could be was a temporary thing. They liked each other, were attracted, and sexually compatible. But he lived in another country.

Evie rested her palm on his chest. She looked at him as though she wanted him to kiss her again. And he wanted to, more than anything.

The words, when they came, were ordinary and matter of fact.

"Could you pass me my robe from the chair?"

She slipped it on and dashed into the bathroom.

Jake leant against the headboard and stared at the ceiling. An irrational impulse tugged at his senses, urging him to take notice. The shower stall was tiny, barely able to contain one person never mind two. He could join her. Not for sex. They didn't have time for that, but he could soap her body, rinse her off.

He squeezed his eyes together to banish the image. Groaned.

"Madness." He voiced the word to dampen his raging libido.

If he stepped into that room, there was no way they'd stop at just one kiss, or just one caress. They'd tumbled into this fuelled by lust. He'd expected that sex would satisfy and dull the constant buzz of attraction he felt when in her orbit, but the opposite was true.

Now he knew how her skin felt beneath his fingertips, how it tasted beneath his lips, the attraction burned brighter than before. Eleanore already thought he had a crush on Evie. Now, a complete stranger would be able to see how involved they were with each other. And Eleanore, who was a master of observation, would tell straight away.

Evie exited the room wrapped in a towel. "Hurry, she'll be home soon."

Jake strode into the bathroom as best he could, holding his clothes in front of his erection. In the shower, he switched the stream of water to cold. And forced himself to stand still under the torrent.

Evie had called Soo while Jake took a shower. They'd always shared important stuff about their lives, so she'd automatically called to share the 'sex with Jake' news. But when the call connected, uncertainty crept in and somehow she couldn't. Instead, she chatted about trivial stuff, with the phone squeezed between her ear and shoulder as though she was doing a yogic shrug. Jake was taking so long in the shower; he must have used up all the hot.

With every drip her ebullient confidence shrunk.

Yes, they'd had great sex. Would he now step back as he had before? She'd been carried away in the moment. Frustrated and attracted. Sure that sex would be the answer. Instead, it was the seed that grew a bunch of questions. She could stay and try to work through them, or—

Evie focused back into their conversation. Soo was explaining she was off to her family's summer house in Connemara for the weekend.

"Can I come too?" The overwhelming sense of relief at potential escape signalled she'd made the right call.

"What about Cleo?"

Eleanore had told her more than once that she'd been quite happy to look after the cat should Evie be away. And Cleo had taught both her and Jake how to look after her.

"She'll be okay." She closed her eyes. "If I'm third wheeling, I understand. It doesn't matter, I just thought—"

"I'm going up alone. The family is there for the weekend, and I've been summoned." She didn't sound delighted about it. Which was crazy, because Soo's family was great. "I would love it if you could come. My brothers don't like Alex. You being there will distract them."

Evie's heart lifted. "Adam and Barnaby are coming?"

"It's a get together of 'The Alphas'."

Evie snorted. Soo's big brothers were known collectively as The Alphas, not because they were Alpha males, but rather because their names started with the first letters of the alphabet. Adam, Barnaby, Charlie, and Damien.

"I need to leave soon. Can you get to mine within an hour?"

"Yes." Evie pulled an overnight bag out from under the bed. "See you there."

She was seated at the table nursing a cup of coffee when the front door opened. Eleanore and the Cinema Girls. Eleanore stuck her head around the kitchen door. "Hi, Evie! Put the kettle on, will you? It's just Rita and me for tea. The others have gone for cocktails."

"Will do."

The girls would settle down in the sitting room, rather than the kitchen. Evie set a tray with cups, saucers, and side-plates. She placed a selection of biscuits on the tray and warmed the teapot.

"I see they're back." Jake stood in the doorway. His hair was damp from the shower and had started to curl a little. She wanted to touch him.

Damn.

"I'm making them tea."

Talk about stating the obvious. But his presence seemed to have sucked all the air from the room. She wanted his hands on her. Wanted his mouth on hers.

116

She swallowed. Put teabags in the pot. Refused to turn around.

"Evie."

So that's what they mean in romance novels when they talk about a man growling a woman's name.

The inane thought surfaced as a haze of lust descended. Then Jake was there, a whisper away. His hand was on her neck, then by some magical move, she was twisted to face him and his mouth was on hers.

She wanted to wrap her arms around him. To twine her legs around his waist like a clinging vine.

The kettle clicked.

"Argh!" She pulled away, placed her hands flat on his chest, and did her best to glower. "Jake, we can't." She pointed to the chair on the other side of the room. "Go. Sit."

He rose one eyebrow. "I'm not a bloody dog, Evie."

"Just do it."

She needed to make the tea, but her hands were still shaking. And if he didn't get out of her orbit she would be in real trouble.

He picked a biscuit off the tray and sprawled on the chair.

She made the tea. "Do you have plans for the weekend?"

One glance told her he'd taken her words as an invitation.

"I want to go away."

Heat in his eyes.

"I've been invited away with Soo, her parents, and The Alphas. I wondered if you and Eleanore could handle looking after Cleo for a couple of days?"

There was a moment's silence. Then Jake stood. He picked up the tray, and she carried the teapot. "Of course, Evie. Anything you want."

Eleanore and Rita had claimed the armchairs. Jake put the tray down on the coffee table and made for the door.

Eleanore checked the tray. "Bring another couple of cups and you two join us."

"I can't, sorry. I need to make a call." He made brief eye contact with Evie. His expression was unreadable.

"You join then, Evie."

Evie felt bruised. Confused. Things had changed in a heartbeat with Jake and she didn't know how she felt about it.

"I will, but just for a moment." She dashed into the kitchen to retrieve a cup. There was no sign of Jake. He must have gone back upstairs.

When she returned to the sitting room, both ladies stopped talking and turned to her. She sank into the 'swallow me up' sofa' with a cup of tea clutched in her hand.

"I asked Jake if he could look after Cleo this weekend—"

"Why would you ask him when you could ask me?" Eleanore smiled.

"Well, he was here, and I needed a quick answer," Evie answered honestly. "I'm off to Connemara with my friend Soo."

"I'll happily look after Cleo. I've told you that before. We can take care of her together, but don't worry, I'll make sure she has everything she needs."

"Thanks so much, Eleanore. I'll be back Sunday evening."

She wanted to believe Jake would take perfect care of Cleo, but it was difficult to trust that men, no matter how charming, would keep to what they'd promised.

And Jake was laser focused on work.

"I have something for you." Eleanore reached for a thick white envelope that lay on the side table nearest her. "I had a chat with Felix's solicitor and asked him to draw up a home share agreement for us. It's boilerplate—essentially the same as he has with his home share friend. I've already signed it, so if you're happy with it, sign both copies and return one to me and we can finalise everything next week. I've put a letter in there detailing the rent and everything. It's what we've already agreed."

Evie took the envelope.

There was a tingle in her nose, and her eyes felt itchy, the way they always did when she was hit by a wave of emotion that made tears threaten.

The constant buzz of worry that she'd pushed down and refused to consider for the past few weeks was silenced with a deep breath. And the knowledge that she had done it. She had found somewhere where she and Cleo could be together and could be safe.

"Thank you." She felt her smile wobble. She clutched the envelope to her chest. "I better go. I don't want Soo to leave without me."

"See you Sunday."

Evie dashed from the room and took the stairs two at a time. She grabbed the case from her bed and tapped on Jake's bedroom door.

"Come."

She left the bag, and the envelope propped up against the wall and opened the door. He was seated at the makeshift desk in the corner, eyeing something on his computer. But stood and strode to her side like a man on a mission.

"I'm going now." She should just go. But her hand crept up to touch the side of his neck. "I'll be back Sunday."

"You're not running away, are you?" His mouth curved into a smile.

She was running away. Running as far away as possible from the possibility of being hurt just as she'd been hurt before. Her mother had warned her not to trust in love, that sharing life with a man meant making yourself vulnerable. When she'd fallen in love with Wyatt, she'd wanted to believe that he wouldn't run at the first sign of trouble. That he'd be at her side as she gave up her life in Dublin to be with her mother and see her through her anguished battle against death.

But he'd proved her mother right by bailing.

Just as her father had on learning of his impending parenthood.

She'd thought she could just have fun with Jake, but after just one night together was realising how deluded she had been with that assumption.

She went up on tiptoe and pressed a kiss against his mouth.

What she'd intended as a quick see you later peck, morphed into something more the instant their lips met. His arms swept around her, pulling her close against his muscular chest as he kissed her so thoroughly her legs wobbled.

Eventually, they broke for air.

"I have to go." She pulled herself from his arms. "I asked Eleanore and she's agreed to look after Cleo."

Before he could respond, she escaped.

Chapter Eighteen

Frustration and irritation burned a hole in Jake's gut. Evie had been gone barely an hour, and already he was missing her presence in the house.

She wanted him as much as he wanted her. But he was definitely right. She was running. He'd known sleeping together would change things, but hadn't expected the changes to happen so quickly.

They'd been floating in a delightful afterglow bubble until he'd gone for his shower. But then, when he'd returned to the room to find her gone, it was as though she'd burst the bubble and erected a wall between them.

She was leaving for the weekend. And he wasn't invited.

There had been no mention of this trip before they'd ended up in bed together, and he'd been mentally shifting work around to make time to take her out again during the weekend. Had been adding pink Tetris Evie pieces into the grid of grey mails, black work, and forest green telephone calls pieces.

He'd been making time for her in his weekend.

She'd been planning a weekend without him.

He was used to being self-sufficient. The last thing he wanted was someone controlling him or demanding more of his time. He should feel relieved to have a solid block of time to brainstorm his final moves in ousting Christopher from Global.

But he missed the taste of her neck.

The smell of her hair.

The touch of her fingers on him.

Her final parting shot had stung. She's already asked him to take care of Cleo and he'd agreed, so why had she then gone to Eleanore and asked the same thing? It suggested she thought him unreliable. Or untrustworthy. Or both.

She'd muttered something about The Alphas. He'd been so stunned that she planned to leave after the afternoon that had thoroughly shaken his world to its foundations that he'd neglected to respond to that particular piece of news.

But now, with nothing to do but analyse every moment of their interaction to see where their relationship had jumped track, he wished she was here so he could question her further.

Who the fuck are the Alphas? A mental picture of a group of Spandex wearing superheroes vying for Evie's attention made acid roil in his stomach.

His phone rang. The screen showed it was Cormac.

"Hey, what's up?" It was a relief to talk to someone. To stop the tormented fantasy scenarios running through his head.

"One of the lads has pulled out at the last minute. Are you any good at football?" Cormac was straight to the point, as always.

"Yeah, not bad." He hadn't played for a couple of years, but he kept his fitness levels up by going to the gym at home.

"What size boots?"

"Eleven."

"Same as me. Great."

"I've no kit."

"I've extra. I'll be over in ten minutes."

~

I've missed them.

Evie hadn't seen all of Soo's family together in one place since her mother's funeral. Before that, she was a constant visitor at their dinner table and had been ever since she and Soo became friends when they were teenagers.

They'd reached out and offered help while Evie was dealing with having to move out of the city and go back home to look after her mum. But she wasn't their responsibility. She wasn't family. So she'd politely demurred.

Maybe that had been the wrong choice.

Soo's mother Meg and father William didn't treat her as a guest. They never had. They treated her as one of their own.

Which is why Meg was piling plates onto her open arms and stacking cutlery and serving tongs on top.

"I don't think I can carry much more."

"You can. Here. Last one." Meg added a huge plastic bottle of ketchup to the top. Then she opened the back door.

Evie staggered out into the sunlight.

"Don't drop anything!"

She stuck her tongue out at Damien, youngest of the Alphas, who was kicking a ball around outside. "Come and help me, you asshole."

He ran over and relieved her of half of her load, which they then deposited on the gingham checked tablecloth of the picnic table William had set up under a giant spreading oak.

A heat haze crinkled the air above the ancient kettle BBQ nearby.

"We need to go back in for more."

Damien danced backwards, palms out. "I'm doing something."

Evie planted her hands on her hips. "Kicking a ball around?" He'd always been an expert at avoiding work. Everyone had stopped even asking Damien to help, because he didn't offer willingly.

He grinned. Shrugged.

"If I'm working, Day, you're working. Come on." She grabbed him by the arm and walked him back to the house.

"You're such a ball buster, you know that? Soo doesn't give me half as bad a time as you do."

"I'm teaching you the essential skills you need to get a girlfriend." Damien was Soo's twin. He had charm by the bucket load and looks that made girls flock to him. But in many ways, he was clueless.

"I have a girlfriend."

Evie blinked. "You do?" She did a pantomime look around from left to right. "Where?"

"Back in Dublin. Smart ass."

She pulled him over to a garden bench half hidden in the undergrowth. They sat. "How long has this been going on?"

"Three months. She's called Sadie. And the reason you haven't heard anything about it is because the family don't know." He frowned and stared into her eyes. "And you're not telling. Not anyone. Not even Soo. Right?"

"Why?" Evie didn't want to keep any secrets from her best friend. Especially not secrets about her twin brother.

"I don't know if you've noticed, but the moment any of this family hear about someone being in a relationship they become consumed with knowing every little detail. Soo's relationship is under the microscope this weekend, which means mine escapes. And that's exactly as I want it."

"Fair enough."

"She's special. I don't want to jinx it."

"Okay."

Damien said he didn't want to talk about Sadie, but didn't seem to be able to help himself. "I like the way I am with her. She sees me in a way my family don't. I don't want to screw up her vision of who I am, if that makes sense? My brothers treat me like a kid. I don't want them judging her."

"I get you." She did. She didn't want to share what was going on in her life with anyone, either. Not even Soo. It was too new, too raw, too difficult to define.

"How are you doing?" There was sympathy in Damien's eyes. He knew how hard the loss of her mother had been. How hard it still was.

"I'm doing okay." It had been a rough eighteen months, but every day got a little easier. "I love my work, and the team I work with. And the past month living with Eleanore has been fun. She's accepted me into her group of friends, and I feel at home there. I've been stressed thinking about finding somewhere for me and the cat, but it's sorted now."

"Listen." His voice lowered. "I don't know if you want to hear this or not, but I promised I'd tell you if I saw you—" Damien's face scrunched up as though he felt he'd be delivering a blow Evie might find painful. "Wyatt's back in Dublin. He asked for your new number."

Evie felt nothing except a vague curiosity.

"I didn't pass it on. I wouldn't unless you want me to." Damien shot Evie a glance, a question in his eyes.

He was friends with both of them. Was in an impossible position. But Evie was glad he'd chosen her side this time.

"No. I don't want to hear from him."

Damien extended an arm and pulled her in to his side on the bench for a hug.

Later, when the meal was finished and everything cleared away, Evie and Soo sat under the oak tree nursing gin and tonics.

"What's going on?" Soo had held back from asking, giving Evie the space she needed on the trip down, but there was no way she could keep her curiosity in check forever. "Did you sleep with him?"

Evie took a deep swallow of her drink. "Yes."

"And?"

"And it was wonderful. So good that I bolted out of the door straight after."

Soo frowned.

"I was pretending to be his girlfriend so the people he'd doing business with will trust him."

Soo's frown deepened. "What the fuck?"

Even the thought of explaining the ins and outs of how this fake relationship began made Evie feel tired. "We've been faking it for a couple of weeks. Then he took me on a date, and we ended up in bed. He's leaving soon. I've just signed a contract to live in his grandmother's house for the next year. I don't know what our relationship is, or what it could be. I just know it's going to be difficult being around him when it all falls apart."

"Maybe it won't all fall apart." Ever the romantic, Soo went for the most positive outcome.

"Maybe." The thought gave her heart a lift.

"Who else thinks you're in a relationship? His grandmother?"

Evie shook her head. "God, no." She thought for a second. "He kissed me in front of Oscar. So everyone at work will be informed by now."

Soo stretched her legs out. "I need to get to know him better."

"I don't think that's a good idea."

"Yeah, well. I do. You needed to be sure about Alex, so I let you give him the first degree when we first started dating. I'm doing the same. We don't know anything about him except that people consider him untrustworthy. Which is a red flag, no matter what he says about it."

The Alphas strode towards them, each carrying a pint of beer. She'd known them all since she was a teenager, and any youthful crushes she might have suffered on any of Soo's brothers had long burned out.

They were a good-looking gang, though.

Adam carried a plaid blanket under his arm. He spread it out before their chairs and the brothers sat.

Soo looked around at her brothers. "Are any of you available on Tuesday night? I'm taking this one out for birthday cocktails in Blazes."

"You are?" Evie was touched. They'd celebrated her birthday last year when they lived together, but she hadn't expected Soo to remember this year.

"Of course I am." Her grin was wide and cheeky. "Bring Jake."

Chapter Nineteen

Jake walked into his bedroom and sat on the bed. He leant against the wall and looked up at the Buzz Lightyear lampshade. This had been his and his brothers' room when they visited. Eleanore had furnished it with kid friendly bedding and a little rug with painted roads on it, which doubled as a racing track for the Matchbox car collection.

Which he hadn't collected. They'd been left in the room for him to play with when he visited. Along with a huge bucket of Lego. She's bought books too. They were probably around here somewhere.

Decades later, all that remained was the lampshade. Part of him wished he was still that kid lying in bed looking up at Buzz and Woody, and dreaming of tomorrow and beyond.

Jake had run out of time.

He groaned and rubbed both hands over his tired face. Lying to everyone was taking a toll.

He'd been in Ireland over a month. Every day, he was dodging telephone calls and avoiding contact with Pat and Christopher. Under normal circumstances, he would have the analysis done, and the contracts signed by now. A fact head office was well aware of.

The more he worked through the documents, the clearer one thing became. That this wasn't just a matter of a company behaving badly. This was information that the guilty would be desperate to keep from getting out. Anyone involved was potentially in danger.

He'd ordered Ellen to stop copying files and made her take a week's holiday to be out of the firing line. She knew it might be longer.

One company, Barden, had suffered catastrophic losses to its workforce. But a cynical, cold-hearted businessman could rightly argue that this was necessary to put the company into profit. And they'd be right. But Jake wasn't taking issue with their practices. He was taking issue with their deceit. They had assured Barden's board that they would preserve the workforce and sell off property holdings to bring the company into line. Jake knew because he'd worked the numbers. He'd sold them that plan.

Only to have everything be reversed the moment the ink on the contract was dry.

He'd been told it had been done in error. That Barden had reconsidered, and decided it was more important to hold on to the real estate, and that they could suffer some redundancies. He'd been lied to—clear and simple. He'd buried his fears and suspicions. Straight after the Barden deal, he'd been put forward as Christopher's successor.

When the next deal was being made, he'd seen the signs with Edjicore. They wanted concrete assurances about not relinquishing control of their company, and he'd told them he couldn't guarantee that.

They'd walked.

There was something rotten in the heart of his company. The only solution was to slice it out. The American parent company needed to be kept in the loop. He spent hours working through every scenario with Suzette and other lawyers in her company. Every scenario, no matter how outlandish had been considered. It was time to act.

Jake stood and took a suitcase from the wardrobe.

This needed to be over.

He'd scored a goal at the match with Cormac's team. And had been treated like a hero in the pub after. The captain had said something about any friend of Cormac's is a friend of ours, and he'd felt raw emotion clutch in his chest.

How could he be a friend if Cormac and Matt knew nothing about what was going on behind the scenes? He wanted to tell them. Wanted to tell Evie everything, too. Keeping secrets felt stifling and toxic. But Suzette had warned of the danger if Christopher and Pat were tipped off too soon.

Evie probably wouldn't be home before he left. He wanted to sit around the kitchen table with her and Eleanore. To celebrate their home share agreement.

He wanted to wrap his arms around her and kiss her senseless.

Instead, she was running, and he was so tightly wound his eyelid was twitching.

Jake made a quick call to Matt and left a voicemail. "I have to close off a couple of things with the team in England, so I won't see you for a few days. Don't sign anything unless I'm with you, okay?"

His message was cryptic, but he couldn't risk Christopher or Pat trying to close the deal behind his back.

He had an appointment with Ben Brookman, CEO of Global at head office in Houston. The accusations he was about to make had the potential to light his career in flames. He needed a witness to every moment of the meeting, so Suzette would be accompanying him.

He placed a call, walking around the room gathering things to place in his suitcase as he spoke to her on speaker.

"My flight gets in at eleven. Will you meet me at the airport?"

"Of course." Her voice was warm and teasing. "Our flight to Houston is so early tomorrow I've booked us in to the airport hotel rather than stay at mine. I hope that suits?"

"It does."

"You've kept everything confidential? It's important the Sweeney brothers don't know what's coming down the line at this stage."

"I feel bad not warning them."

"There's nothing you can do right now." Suzette was quiet for a long moment. "I'm sorry, Jake. But you know we must do this. Once we put this thing in motion, there's no going back. Your friendships may well be over. I better go. See you soon."

"See you at arrivals, Suzette."

Evie's feet were rooted to the spot. She'd just come back from Connemara. Hadn't even had a chance to change clothes before Eleanore met her at the door with a giant smile and a pitcher of icy pink sludge.

"Felix is taking me out to dinner, but I want us to celebrate before I go. Jake's upstairs. Can you fetch him?"

His door was open a fraction. Enough that she could hear the entire conversation with him, and some woman called Suzette.

She was picking him up tonight from the airport and tomorrow they were flying to America. They were keeping secrets. Secrets he didn't want Matt and Cormac made aware of.

Every breath was a struggle.

She'd fought against trusting him. Had finally overcome her fears and gone to bed with him, knowing she was in too deep to be able to brush off their encounter as just casual. She'd thought him worth the risk.

Idiot.

She rubbed her eyes. Walked back to the top of the stairs and took a steadying breath.

Don't let them know how much they've hurt you.

Some of the floorboards on the landing creaked. She stepped on every single one on the way to rapping on his door.

Jake opened the door.

She plastered on a bright smile. "Eleanore needs us both downstairs."

"I'll just—" He reached for her hand, but she danced back out of reach.

"See you down there."

Eleanore sat at the kitchen table. She'd made a cake and iced it in pink icing. E + E was marked out on the top in Jelly Tots.

"We need to celebrate the next stage in both of our lives. I want to celebrate our living together."

Evie stared down at the pastel jelly sweets. "Evie and Eleanore. I love it."

"There wasn't enough room for anything else." Eleanore had set out three cocktail glasses on the kitchen table. "Rita brought me some strawberries from her garden, and you know what they say about if life gives you lemons."

Evie felt her brow pleat.

"Make lemonade, dear. I'm working on the 'if Rita gives you strawberries make strawberry daiquiris', principle."

"Good thinking." Alcohol. That would help.

She heard the door behind her open. Didn't look around as Eleanore greeted Jake. Instead, she busied herself pouring the cock-tail into three glasses.

She handed one to Jake and one to Eleanore. "I'll cut the cake?"

Her hands were busy with the cake. The pink icing was the old type, the type her mother used to make. Icing sugar and water, making a thin glaze rather than thick buttercream. It fractured and split into shards as she cut.

The little jellied sweets were covered in sugar. A couple shifted when she moved a slice onto a plate. Leaving circular holes behind. Eleanore and Jake were talking. She tried to block the sounds out.

When the plates were distributed, she had no option but to sit down and join the conversation.

The strawberry daiquiri was half rum.

"Good drink." She raised her glass. Drank again.

"I'm flying to England tonight. A car will be here to take me to the airport in a few minutes." Jake spoke to both of them but looked at Evie.

"Oh?"

"That's short notice, dear. How long will you be away?" Eleanore asked.

Tell us about flying on to America. Tell us about Suzette. Make this make sense. Don't let me be wrong about you.

"Just a few days. There's some business at the office I need to take care of."

A car's horn sounded from outside. Jake checked his watch. "Damn, that's them." He shoved the rest of his slice of cake into his mouth, chewing furiously.

"Oh, seeing as you have a car right now, could you give me a lift to Felix's flat? It's on the way."

Jake nodded. Rushed to the window and waved to the driver that he was coming, then disappeared upstairs to fetch his luggage.

"I'm sorry you're going to be on your own tonight, Evie."

Eleanore put on her coat and took her bag from the hook near the door.

"No problem. Have a good night."

Evie poured herself another drink. Eleanore had made enough for a party. It would be a party of one.

Chapter Twenty

The next few days passed in a blur. Last year, Evie had worked her birthday, and regretted it. One of the guides made it his mission to tell the visitors, which meant that every tour involved large amounts of plastic helmet touting Vikings roaring directly at her.

By the time she left work, her head had been pounding.

So, at the beginning of the year, when people were marking out their holiday days, she'd put in to have her birthday off.

The days since Jake left for the airport had been hard. She'd cried off her salsa class with Soo and had spent as little time as possible with Eleanore. Anyone who knew her, who cared for her, would be able to see that something was wrong.

Maybe she'd misheard. Maybe he hadn't decided to fly to Houston with Suzette. Perhaps he hadn't lied to her face.

She rang his UK office and asked to talk to him.

His secretary told her he was working with a client in Ireland and therefore unavailable. Could she take a message?

Evie declined and hung up.

Whatever he and the mysterious woman were doing was not sanctioned by his office. He'd gone rogue.

Soo had left messages, asking if she was okay. She hadn't had the energy to respond, or the desire to lie. Birthday drinks were booked for tonight. She must make an excuse to cancel.

Evie pulled the duvet over her head. She closed her eyes. Her mother used to say, "You can have whatever you want on your birthday."

She knew what she wanted. She wanted to wind back time to the moment before Jake turned out to be an asshole.

But then, that wouldn't work. Because he'd still be an asshole, she'd just be oblivious.

She wanted...

She wanted...

Whoever the hell was stabbing her doorbell repeatedly to stop.

Evie threw back her duvet and pulled on a ratty robe. She strode to the door and peeked through the spyhole.

Soo was on the doorstep.

Evie opened the door.

"No work?"

"It's my birthday present to myself." Evie turned and walked into the kitchen.

"What's going on?" Soo put down a bag of croissants on the table.

Evie made coffee. "I can't go tonight. You'll have to cancel."

"What the hell?" Soo grabbed her shoulders, turned her around. "The Alphas are all set. I raided your contacts list, contacted Lisa Sweeney and she, Matt, and Cormac are coming. She asked if Jake would be back from England by then."

She frowned. "Is he in England? You only had to invite one person. Did you?"

"It's over." Evie opened the fridge and retrieved a large bar of fruit and nut chocolate. "He doesn't know it's over, but it's over."

"So you're done with him, and he doesn't know?" Soo sat and ran her hands through her shiny black bob. "When are you going to learn to communicate?"

That was bloody harsh.

Evie stuffed another few cubes of chocolate into her mouth.

"You're allowed to ask for things you want. You're allowed to show your feelings when you're hurt. You don't have to be a bloody robot."

Evie shot to her feet. "Where the hell do you get off talking to me like that?" She poked her fingers into Soo, leaving a sticky brown chocolate mark on the front of Soo's T-shirt.

"That's it." Soo's satisfied smile stoked the fire inside Evie. "You need to be angry, not sad."

"You're manipulating me. I want you to leave."

"Not going to happen." The smile faded from Soo's face. "I love you. You know that." She grasped Evie's wrist and tugged her down to sitting again. She breathed in and out a few times, getting ready to deliver more harsh words. "I need to talk about Wyatt."

Evie's eyebrows rose.

"He's useless, okay? He talked about rent when he should have been talking about what you needed from him. That's partly his fault, but it's also yours. You didn't tell him how you felt about his reaction. You told me how hurt you felt. How you wanted him to support you and tell you he'd be with you every step of the way. But you never told him. You don't open yourself up to discussion."

Evie stared into her coffee cup.

"You have to talk about it, Evie. Feeling pain and showing it doesn't make you weak, it makes you human."

"I thought I was in love with Jake." Surprise flickered through Evie as she spoke the words. Was it really love? "I know I needed to communicate rather than running, so I went back. I went back for him."

"What happened?"

"I heard him talking to a woman on speakerphone and making a plan to get on a plane to Houston with her. Seems like the Sweeneys were right to be cautious of Jake. He's been lying to all of us." Evie's chest squeezed as though compressed in a vice. Her eyes stung. Haltingly, she recounted the rest of conversation she'd overheard.

Soo's eyes flashed. She glanced at her phone. "Houston."

Evie managed a nod.

"It's nine thirty here, which makes it," she checked her phone. "about three thirty in the morning in Houston. Give me his number."

Soo punched in the digits. Placed the phone on the table on speaker. There was an unfamiliar ringtone, and eventually the phone was picked up.

"Yello?"

Jake's familiar voice was thick with sleep.

"Jake, is it?" Soo asked, her voice artificially bright and breezy. "This is Evie's friend, Soo."

"Is Evie okay?" He was one hundred per cent awake in an instant.

"Oh, yeah. Sure, she's fine. I got your number from her phone. I know you're in England at the moment." She pulled a 'like hell you are' face. "Anyway, I'm calling you about tonight. You probably know it's Evie's birthday, and I've organised a party in a club. I know she'd want you to be there."

There was silence for a long moment.

"She didn't tell me." The silence stretched. "I can't make it. Work is killing me at the moment. I can't be there. I'll make it up to her when I get back."

Soo was clenching her teeth so hard her jawline flexed.

"Okay, well. Good talking to you!" She stabbed the hang up icon.

She wrapped her arm around Evie's shoulder. "I'm sorry for giving you a hard time. I'm staying with you all day today. And tonight, we're getting dressed up and going to your party where you're going to have the best damn time of your life."

Soo reached into her bag and pulled out a box wrapped in pink paper and holographic ribbon. "Here. Try on your present."

~

Getting a meeting with the owner of Global Innovations was harder than Jake had imagined. Ben Brookman bounced their scheduled meeting, citing pressure of work.

Jake and Suzette had been stuck in a hotel suite for days, waiting for a rescheduled meeting to take place.

Today's the day.

They walked shoulder to shoulder into the sumptuous penthouse office.

Dramatic modern paintings in primary colours hung on white walls. The floor was a shining expanse of Carrara marble.

Ben stood from behind a huge modern glass and metal desk and walked around to shake their hands.

"Sorry to keep you waiting." He acted as though they'd been waiting for minutes, rather than for days. "I was in discussions with the government. You know how politicians can be."

He gestured to a suite of armchairs and a coffee table in the other corner of the room. "Let's sit."

"I'd like to record this conversation, if that's okay with you." Suzette held her phone.

Ben's gaze shot to Jake. "What's this about?"

"Allegations of corruption. There are things going on in the UK office you're not aware of."

Ben held up a hand, palm out. He opened the door and spoke to his secretary. "Get my lawyer up here now."

He walked back to the chairs and sat. "Good move, bringing your legal counsel. I'm sure you won't begrudge me the same. He shouldn't be long. Coffee?"

Twenty minutes later, Ben left the room to consult with his

lawyer. They walked into the room as if they were opposing counsel, rather than on the same team.

Suzette's shoulders were stiff as she shook hands. She didn't smile.

"We shall both record this conversation." Ben waited until both lawyers primed their recording devices and placed them on the coffee table. "Ready?" He waved at Jake. "Go ahead."

"I've learned that Christopher Jones and Pat Wiley have conspired to keep information from the companies we've acquired. They have given verbal guarantees they have no intention of honouring."

Ben looked bored.

His lawyer spoke, "Unsavoury, but not illegal."

"They've also conspired to keep me out of the loop. We have emails between Christopher and Pat where they discuss hiding information from me so that I will close these deals while not in full possession of the facts. That's fraud."

Suzette pulled a file from her briefcase.

"Technically—" Ben's lawyer started.

Jake cut him off. "I've fought for transparency and honour my entire business life. I believe in Global. I believe our company motto: that together we're stronger. With Christopher's retirement due soon, I'd hoped he might step down early and Pat could be encouraged to seek alternative employment. Unfortunately, our investigation has led us to believe this is a far bigger problem than just casual lies."

He took the file from Suzette.

"Initial investigations have identified five companies that have been fraudulently misled. There needs to be a full independent enquiry."

"There is some suggestion that payments may have been made." Suzette spoke carefully.

"May I?" Ben's lawyer reached for the file.

"These are very serious allegations." Ben steepled his fingers.

"Christopher has worked for Global for decades. I like to think of him as a friend."

"The paper trail doesn't lie."

"Have you spoken to him about this?" Ben asked.

"No." Why was Ben even asking that? Surely he understood—

"Christopher always says you're an idealist." Ben smiled as though talking indulgently to a child. "Idealists don't always like to examine the minutiae of running a huge company like ours. The law's the law, and it's important not to do anything illegal. But sometimes you must get your hands dirty."

Ben glanced at his lawyer.

"This meeting is over." He stood and crossed his hands behind his back. "Thanks for coming in. We'll be in touch."

Jake and Suzette gathered their things. They stood in silence in the elevator and didn't exchange so much as a word until they were in a cab back to their hotel.

"He's in on it." They'd brainstormed this scenario. Jake hadn't wanted to believe that the rot extended all the way up to the top of the organisation. He'd held on to hope that the corruption was contained to one office. But Ben's response was unequivocal.

Christopher was following his boss's orders.

"Plan B, then?"

Suzette agreed.

Jake had handed the file to Ben's lawyers. There was no doubt they'd be locating and destroying documents before he and Suzette were even back in their hotel. "Did you hand over everything?"

Suzette shook her head. "Copies of some emails, but nothing significant. They won't know which servers they should scrub as a matter of priority. We have some time, but not much."

Jake called down for a cab. They'd packed for their flight the night before and left their luggage next to the door, ready to go.

Suzette reached into her bag and grabbed her mobile. "I'll brief our team. They'll pass the files to the City of London Police and get the SFO involved."

Chapter Twenty-One

Soo and Evie had been going to the Blaze Club ever since college. The building was set out over four floors, but the second floor was their favourite. This floor was for get togethers, rather than dancing. The music was muted, and small tables filled the space. The walls and ceilings were painted midnight blue with twinkling stars set into the ceiling.

The mirrored bar was set with bottles of every possible alcoholic drink and highlighted in pink neon. It was so eighties you could almost imagine Tom Cruise and Bryan Brown flipping cocktail shakers around.

Soo had booked the VIP area, which was just three large tables set up on a dais behind a velvet rope in the corner of the room. The guests she'd invited had yet to arrive. Or maybe they'd stopped on the lower floor for a dance.

Evie sat alone at the top table.

Soo clicked over on high heels.

"I'm having sex on the beach."

Not even Soo's regular cocktail-based innuendo could raise a smile.

Evie raised her glass. "Mojito for me. Third mojito, actually."

The alcohol didn't seem to be having any effect at all. She picked out a mint leaf and chewed.

"How's it going?" Soo looked concerned.

"Better than expected. You were right. I needed to get out." There was only so much hiding under a duvet a woman can do. Once she'd heard Jake on the phone brushing Soo off and doubling down on his lie, something inside had changed. She'd stopped feeling weak and tearful and had switched to determined.

Soo's words earlier had been difficult to hear.

But maybe she was right. Maybe instead of taking the pain and hiding her reaction, it would be cathartic to honestly respond.

She wouldn't even think about him now. Wouldn't waste a minute on what ifs.

"Jake will be in my life for the next year, whether I like it or not because I'm living with Eleanore." She clinked her glass against Soo's. "When he comes back, I'm going to tell him how I feel. I've had it with lying, of pretending I'm not in pain."

Soo tapped her hand. "The Sweeneys."

Matt, Cormac, and Lisa were being directed to their position by a bouncer. They clutched presents and looked excited to be out.

Evie stood to greet them. The hostess unfastened the velvet rope to allow them entry.

Lisa grabbed her into a hug. The men did likewise. Evie felt emotion threaten to overwhelm. They were such good people. So natural and honest about their feelings. They didn't deserve whatever scummy thing Jake was doing to them.

Matt looked around. "Is Jake not here?"

"No." She couldn't cover for him. "I'm sorry. I know you're here because you work with him, but Jake and I—"

She choked.

Soo took over. "They're having some problems right now." She called a waiter over. "Let's get some drinks."

"Sit yourself down, babe." Lisa took over as the others gave their orders to the waiter. "Are you okay?"

I'm done pretending I'm not in pain.

"Not really. I don't know what's going on. Jake isn't in London. He's in America."

Lisa glanced across at her husband and his brother. Gave come here gestures with her hand. They pulled chairs close.

"Say that again," Lisa said.

"Jake told me he was going to the London office. But he isn't there. I overheard him on the phone talking with a woman and planning to fly to Houston."

"Texas?" Lisa squeaked.

"Global's head office is in Texas." Cormac frowned.

"He told us not to sign anything." Matt pulled his cell from his pocket. "What do you think's going on, Evie?"

All three looked at Evie, as though she held the answer to Jake's mysterious behaviour. They thought they were a couple, that they were in love and that he would have confided in her.

"I don't know." She swallowed. "We exaggerated our relationship." She looked at Cormac. "Jake was concerned you didn't trust him. When Lisa presumed we were a couple we didn't contradict her." She gritted her teeth. "I'm sorry. I like you guys. I'm sorry for misleading you."

"I thought you were in a relationship." Disappointment was all over Lisa's face.

Soo stepped in. "They were. It started out as fake, but by the time they went to your wedding renewal their relationship was becoming real."

"Soo, what the hell—"

"It was. Don't deny it. I know you."

Evie looked from Matt to Cormac. "He went to Houston with some woman. He said he wanted to tell you guys what was going on, but she advised against it."

Matt planted his hands on his hips. "We need to talk to him. Right now. Come on, Lisa."

Evie touched Lisa's arm as she made to walk past them. "I'm sorry, Lisa."

"The rest of it's true, right? You live with his grandmother and drive the Duck?"

"Yes, that's all true. The only thing we lied about was how long we'd known each other and that we were a couple."

With a terse nod, Lisa followed Cormac and Matt from the room. Nerves clutched at Evie's stomach. If Jake wasn't running a con, if instead he was trying to save the Sweeney brothers' company, she had just blown the whole thing wide open.

She might have just destroyed his life.

Something across the room caught her eye. Despite the severity of the situation, she couldn't hold back a smile.

A group strode towards the VIP area. Adam and Damien carried either end of a banner reading *Happy Birthday* in neon yellow. All the Alphas wore matching white sleeveless T-shirts which clung to their impressive chests. Each had a letter emblazoned in neon yellow on the front.

E.V.I.E.

They all wore feather boas.

Barnaby carried a birthday cake.

A waitress clearing glasses from the table paused to take in the view. She scanned each Alpha head to toe, like someone considering an expensive purchase, then grinned at Evie. "Wow. Who are they?"

Adam was close enough to hear.

"We're her brothers." Thin paper streamers filled the air from countless enthusiastically pulled party poppers. "Happy Birthday, Evie!"

Jake was so exhausted he could barely keep his eyes open. He and Suzette had been met by her colleague at Heathrow arrivals and were taken straight to an interview with the Serious Fraud Office.

Suzette sat at his side as he went through all the documentation and proof with the SFO investigator. They then had to discuss who definitely was involved and who might be.

After that, he had to give a written statement.

He and Suzette shared an Uber.

When they reached her home, Suzette climbed out and talked to Jake through the open window while the Uber driver unloaded her luggage. "The City of London police need you to stay in the country for the next few days."

"I need to get home."

Suzette looked at him blankly. His home was the next stop.

"I mean Dublin. I need to get back to my grandmother's house."

"Not for a few days." Suzette took her bag from the driver. "Talk to you tomorrow."

Jake had taken a panicked call from Matt en route. He'd revealed that Evie had told them about his lies. That she knew he was in Houston, rather than London. She knew he was involved in something, but didn't know what.

Evie wouldn't answer his calls or respond to his texts. He didn't blame her. He wouldn't trust him either, given the evidence. He needed to speak to her face to face.

The Uber delivered him to his flat. He walked in and strode into the sitting room to crash on the sofa in the dark.

He pulled out his phone. Rang Eleanore. Then lay down on the sofa.

"What's going on, Jake?" She didn't bother with pleasantries. "Evie's upset. She says she doesn't want to talk about it, but I think it has something to do with you."

"Is she there?"

Eleanore was silent for a moment. "She's upstairs. If you wanted to talk to her, why did you call me?"

"She won't answer the phone to me."

Eleanore blew out a breath. "If she won't answer the phone to you, she doesn't want to talk to you. That's not difficult to understand."

"I've been lying to her." There was a sour taste in Jake's mouth. He covered his eyes with his forearm. "It's complicated."

"I've nothing but time, son. Let's hear it."

An hour later, Jake hung up.

Jetlag was setting in. A rolling nausea brought on by too many hours since sleep and the close confines of the SFO office. His body clock considered the time as night, but it was still daytime.

He flicked on the kettle. Walked into the bathroom and turned on the shower. The Sweeneys had been shocked and disappointed to hear what was going on. He'd promised a thorough debrief over Zoom when he could.

There was no time like the present.

Chapter Twenty-Two

Evie quite liked stag parties. Not late in the evening, obviously. Because no one liked lads out on a stag do once they'd drunk the city dry and become obnoxious. But earlier in the day, before they started drinking, they were different animals.

The nine friends who'd booked the Duck this afternoon were sober. They'd decided on a gladiator theme, and all looked fantastic in white shortie togas with chestnut leather breastplates, red cloaks, and leather strap sandals. Oscar had confiscated their swords and stowed them for safety.

The Viking helmets were the wrong era but added a fun touch.

One of the stag boys had decided to sit as close as possible to Evie and chat.

"Jonno's missus to be has a thing for gladiators. Well, I don't know if it's gladiators or guys with eight packs. She's keener on Gerard Butler and his Spartans than Russell Crowe, if you know what I mean."

Evie did. She muttered agreement and steered around a corner.

"You know they should have called that movie *2400*. Because three hundred times eight packs—"

Oscar leant in. "Eighteen hundred, mate. That's what it's known as. Six packs are more achievable."

"Jonno's six pack isn't the best." Stag boy sounded sincere, rather than critical. "He wants to give her photos of himself dressed up and was worried he'd fall short. But we have it all sorted."

"You do?" Evie shouted, without taking her eyes off the road.

"After this, we're getting fake tan abs done. He thought he might look ridiculous, so we all signed up. We're all in the same boat, eh?"

He laughed at his own joke.

"I need to ask you to sit further back so I can consult with the driver for a minute," Oscar said.

He ushered the passenger down the Duck and returned to the front seat.

"Consult?"

"I thought you could do with a break. I sure could." Oscar unwrapped a mint from the packet Evie stored in the dash and ate it.

"They're sweet though. They all really care about him."

Oscar glanced back at the group. "He'll remember this his whole life. Not for the party or the costumes, but because his best friends showed they had his back. That they were his family."

They pulled up to the dock. Evie turned off the engine while the floatation devices were attached to the Duck's sides, and the passengers put on their life jackets.

"Are you okay, Evie?" Oscar said in a quiet voice. "You've been quiet the past couple of days. Is everything okay with you and Jake?"

"No. Not really." Talking about her feelings was difficult at the best of times. And right now really wasn't a good time.

"I saw all that stuff in the newspapers."

"Me too." The news cycle had been on repeat, pushing two different narratives. One, the story being put out by Global, was that Jake Ridley was a rogue employee with a grudge trying to destroy the company. The other touted him as a brave whistle-blower trying to bring down a corrupt behemoth. "I don't know what to believe."

"Have you talked to him?"

She'd talked to Eleanore. And every member of the John Woo Appreciation Society had an opinion they'd been eager to share.

"Not yet. He's returning this afternoon."

The floatation devices were on. The helpers stood back.

"Are we ready to take to the water?" Oscar shouted.

The answering roar was deafening.

The rest of the tour went as planned. Evie stood next to Oscar as the passengers disembarked, handing out shields as Oscar rearmed them with their plastic swords.

"Have a good night. No, I'm sorry, I can't." Evie demurred in response to the flurry of suggestions that flew her way. That she should join them. That she and Oscar could get their abs painted on with fake tan too and party until dawn.

As they sauntered off down the side of Stephen's Green, the gladiators drew glances, double takes, and smiles.

"Ah. to be young and in love." Oscar locked up the back. "You want a lift?"

Every particle in her body urged her to delay. To kill time window shopping or visiting a friend. But she couldn't put off going home forever. And when she did, he'd be waiting.

"That would be great, thanks."

The house was silent when she entered. She hung her coat, kicked off her boots, and walked into the kitchen in search of Cleo.

Eleanore sat on a kitchen chair with the cat on her lap. She wore her raincoat and an interesting hat in a dark plum shade that might have been knitted by someone in her class.

"What's up?" Evie walked over and stroked Cleo.

"I'm waiting."

Evie waited for more. It wasn't forthcoming.

"What are you waiting for, Eleanore?"

"I'm waiting for Felix."

Evie sank onto a chair.

"He asked me to go away with him on a mini break." She glanced down to a holdall next to the chair. "He's picking me up any minute."

"A mini break. That sounds awesome. Where are you going?"

"We're going to stay in a hotel in Wexford. I haven't told Jake, and he's due any minute too. I'm hoping to be out of here before he arrives."

"What do you want me to tell him?"

Cleo jumped off Eleanore's lap and started miaowing at the fridge, as if it were a sentient being, able to open at will and dispense ham, rather than controlled by the house's occupants.

"I suppose you'll just have to tell him I'm away with my fancy man." She squeezed her hands together. "I don't want to disillusion the boy. He's such a romantic."

Evie's eyes widened. "Really?"

"He doesn't do casual. Never has, according to his mother. I don't want him to get the wrong idea about me and Felix. I have no intention of living with him, or of getting married. I've been there, done that. I'm not sure my grandson would like to know that I've a friend with benefits, though."

The doorbell rang. Felix stood on the doorstep dressed in three-piece tweed. Before Evie could invite him in, Eleanore was there at her side. "Could you bring my things to the car, dear?"

She kissed Felix's cheek.

"Tell him." Her gaze was serious with unstated undertones. "I'll be back in a week." She squeezed Evie's hand. "Everything will be okay."

~

Tension left Jake's shoulders the moment he unlocked the front door and stumbled into the house. He dumped his bags. Breathed in deep. Closed his eyes.

He was home.

He hadn't had this feeling when he returned to his rented apartment. Amid his belongings, he'd felt like a visitor. All he had in his bedroom in this house were a couple of shirts, the contents of a laundry hamper, and a paperback. He glanced to the stick box just inside the door. Strode over and rooted through the contents till he found it. Jake's shillelagh. Left here when he was a kid and never thrown away.

Just as he'd left some part of himself here as a kid. An echo. A memory of a moment, of himself. His gaze shifted to the pictures on the wall. Fading photographs of him and his brothers. One of him knitting with the same pink needles he'd taught Evie on.

This was home. Not for the pictures or the stick, but for the people. For Eleanore, who'd loved him all his life. And Evie who he hoped might.

There was a sound emanating from further inside the house. A high, bright, joyful sound he didn't ever remember hearing in the house before.

Jake walked down the hall to the closed door of the sitting room. He turned the knob and pushed the door open.

The sound died.

Evie stood at the harp, both hands wide and flattened to silence the strings.

"You're here." She didn't move.

"I didn't know you played."

"I don't." She tilted the harp from her shoulder and walked around it to the sofa. "I mean, I know a couple of songs, but I'm no expert."

"Will you play for me?"

Evie shook her head. "I don't play for people." One corner of her mouth lifted in a rueful smile. "I rarely play for animals."

Jake sat on the sofa. The cat was between them. She purred and started testing her nails on his thigh.

"You were playing, though." He eased a fingertip between Cleo's nails and his jeans in a fruitless attempt to remain unscratched.

"Mum used to play to cheer me up, back before she became ill." She stroked Cleo's head. "I thought it was time to bring back some good memories." Her gaze flicked up to his. "I told the Sweeneys you were a liar. That you couldn't be trusted."

"I know." The brothers had explained everything. Including how devastated she'd appeared at learning what she'd considered the truth. "I'm sorry. I wanted to tell you. I've screwed everything up but I—"

Evie stood and changed seats, so she was sitting in the armchair opposite.

"I need to tell you how I feel about everything. I know it's not all about me, but it will be all about me until I'm finished."

"I—"

"I don't want you to interrupt me." A vein in the corner of her jawline flexed. "I just want you to listen."

Jake waited.

"I was a happy kid. I never met my father and never want to. My mother was enough. She was alone in the world before she had me. She loved my father and was disappointed when he bailed before I was even born. She used to say, never let them see you cry. Don't give them the satisfaction."

She held up a hand when it looked as though he might interrupt.

"I don't want any pity. I'm okay with all this. I'm just trying to explain *me*."

Jake tried to show he was attentive, understanding and encouraging, without nodding his head constantly like a bobble headed figure or speaking, which she didn't seem to be a fan of currently.

"When I had to leave college, my boyfriend and I broke up. I closed off and never told him how I felt. I run rather than face emotion. Because I'm scared."

It was taking all he had not to walk over there and take her in his arms.

"So after we slept together, I ran. I didn't know how I felt about you, didn't know if you and I could have something real, or if I'd be hurt again." She crossed her arms. "I decided to risk it. I came back. That's when I heard you talking to Suzette on speaker, and you lied to my face." Her throat worked. "I can't trust you."

"Suzette's my lawyer." He blurted before she could stop him. She needed to know that the relationship he had with the other woman wasn't anything personal.

"Lisa rang to tell me that."

"I tried to tell you, but you wouldn't answer your phone."

Evie's shoulders stiffened. "You asked me to pretend to be in a relationship with you for the Sweeney brothers. I couldn't tell when you were acting and what was real. One minute you were hot, the next you were cold. All that deceit is another strike against you."

He nodded again. Bobble headed. He felt decidedly bobble headed.

"Despite it all, I love you." She blew out a breath, visibly deflating. "I don't want to be with someone I can't trust, so I don't know what that even means."

"Can I talk now?"

She crossed her arms and leant back, waiting.

"You love me."

"That's all you got from what I said?"

"That's the most important."

"I disagree." She looked the most serious he'd ever seen him. "There needs to be honesty. There needs to be trust. There needs to be—"

"Communication." Frustration made his voice harsh. "Even before you knew there was a problem, you ran away from me, Evie.

I thought I was making the right decision by keeping you in the dark about the shit that was going down in the company, but I was wrong. I distanced myself when I should have opened up and been honest. I understand you have relationship issues. I do too. But lecturing me and not letting me talk back isn't the way to heal things. I want to try to see a way through for us. A relationship is give and take. I've made mistakes, but I need you to listen to me. I want to be with you."

Evie looked to the window. People were walking past on the pavement. Living their lives. Her body language shouted she wanted to join them. To be anywhere other than here.

"People have relationships without happy ever after love. Your grandmother could tell you all about that."

Jake listened to the silent house. "Where is Eleanore anyway? Out at one of her social things?"

"She's gone away for a few days with Felix." She fixed him with an intent gaze. "She and Felix are what you might call dating. She doesn't know how to tell you because she thinks you might judge her because they're more than friends. If you know what I mean."

'She and Felix?" It all slotted into place. Felix was often there for dinner, and she spent one night a week playing poker at his home. Jake presumed they were platonic friends, but on reflection the fact that they were more was obvious. "Are they thinking of moving in together?" Might there even be a wedding in Eleanore's future?

Evie stood and started pacing around the room. "She said you'd be like this. That you'd start to imagine they were in love and getting married. Eleanore says that's not what she wants. She and Felix are friends. They enjoy each other's company. They like being together. She told me she had her big love, and Felix had his. Neither of them is looking for that again. They make each other happy, and that's enough."

"Evie—"

"Eleanore's away for the week. I don't know how I feel, but

right now I don't have anything more to talk to you about. We're both living here, but I'd appreciate it if you could stay out of my way."

She made for the door. And in a matter of seconds, he was alone again.

Chapter Twenty-Three

J ake left Evie alone, just as she'd asked. She came back from work the following day to a note on the kitchen table telling her he would be back in the hotel until Eleanore was back home. He added if she wanted him for anything, she only needed to call or send a text.

She wanted him for everything. And not calling or telling him to come home felt like ripping her chest open and pummelling her heart. She'd told him she loved him but couldn't trust him.

The colours seemed to have washed out of life without him.

She went to her dancing class with Soo and could barely raise a smile even when the salsa dance teacher suffered a costume malfunction. It had only been three days, but time stretched out as if it were forever. Without Eleanore and her diverse group of friends, the house was cold and silent. There must be a way forward, but she couldn't find it.

On a whim, she'd called Damien and given him the okay to pass her number on to Wyatt.

Which is how she found herself sitting in a bar they'd used to frequent years ago, back when they were a couple. She'd got there early. The table they always used to sit was available, so she'd chosen it. He always sat on the right. She on the left, with a good view of the door to monitor the goings on.

Back then, she would have ordered beer. Now, she ordered vodka.

Nerves danced in her stomach every time the door swung open. When Wyatt's familiar outline came into frame, a wave of mixed emotion flooded her.

She stood.

He strode over, clutched her upper arms and kissed both cheeks. "Hey, you." His smile was warm and welcoming. He looked fit and tanned. Gorgeous as ever.

"I ordered."

"I'll get myself one."

She sat down and smoothed her palms over her pale pink summer dress. Idly checked out Wyatt's back view as he stood at the bar. In minutes, he was back at the table. Sitting across from her.

"I haven't been here since we split." He lifted his pint and clinked it against her glass. "I can't even count the number of times we sat at this table."

"I know. I haven't been here since either." She'd walked past plenty of times but had never ventured inside. It seemed wrong, somehow, as if it were a place belonging to another her, from another time.

"Thanks for letting Damien give me your number. I really wanted to see you." He reached across the table as if reaching for her hand. Then he stopped. Curled his fingers into his palm. "I felt there was unfinished business between us."

His earnest blue gaze held hers. Once upon a time, she couldn't imagine spending her life without him. Now, she couldn't imagine spending even a day with him.

"I've moved on. Obviously." A wry grin teased the edge of his mouth. "And I know you have too. This isn't an attempt to relight our fire."

"Good." She swallowed a mouthful of her drink. "I'm on the same page as you about that."

"I've always felt bad about how we ended things. You were a huge part of my life, and I loved you. When we broke up, you just brushed it off as though it were nothing." A shadow passed across his face. "I let my hurt and anger keep me from coming to your mother's funeral. For reaching out. I wanted to tell you I was sorry."

He'd hurt her. But Soo was right, she'd hurt him right back.

She reached her hand out and placed it over his.

"I'm sorry too. Leaving you wasn't nothing. What we had wasn't nothing."

She could feel the tension in his body radiating through his clenched knuckles.

Wyatt cleared his throat. "I could have handled it better. But when you told me you'd quit college and were walking out on me, I didn't know how to react. I wasn't expecting it, you know? I just saw everything in my life blowing up and there wasn't a damn thing I could do about it."

Evie squeezed his hand and released it.

"There was no discussion. No chance to work through the problems facing us as a couple. You kept me in the dark, made your decisions, and moved right on."

Evie winced. She didn't want to think that she had acted that way, but he was right. She'd seen a problem and acted and not factored Wyatt in at all.

She clasped her hands together. "You're right, I did do that. I've never acknowledged that even to myself. I thought my mother's illness was my problem, rather than ours. I did exactly what my mother did my whole life. I acted alone. "

Wyatt rubbed the back of his neck. Rotated his shoulders. Body language cues he'd always used to show he was trying to dissipate tension.

"I presented you with a done deal and didn't take into account the shock that must have been. My mum used to tell me to put my bright side out. That showing vulnerability was wrong. She pleaded for my father to stay, and he left anyway. Leaving you, blowing up my life, was the most difficult thing I'd ever had to do. I thought telling you how I felt would make me weak. Would make me vulnerable. I never let you see that, and I'm sorry too. Sorry I didn't trust you and us enough to show you how I really felt. I loved you too."

Wyatt ran his hands through his mop of blond hair. "I'm shaking."

"Me too." Evie looked at her hands. Her fingers looked steady, but inside she felt unsettled. Wobbly. "I guess we both needed this. Closure."

"Closure. Sure. Maybe closing off unfinished business and opening a new phase of our relationship. I've missed having you as a friend, Evie. Since I've been back, I've met up with Damien and the rest of the Alphas and I'd have loved you and Soo to be there, too. But, of course, Soo won't talk to me—"

"She will now." They used to all hang out together, back then. She'd gone home to look after her mother. Wyatt had gone to Germany. The Alphas had scattered with the wind. Now, for a brief moment in time, they were all back in Dublin. Back in each other's lives. Maybe they could rebuild.

"So tell me," she teased. "Have you someone new in your life?"

The thought of being in the same house as Evie and having to avoid her was unthinkable. So the morning after their discussion, Jake had done what any reasonable person would have done. He'd given her space. He'd left the house the next morning with a few things thrown into an overnight bag. The prospect of moving back into the sterile, unwelcoming hotel room was unappealing but necessary.

He'd check in later.

But first he needed to have a face-to-face meeting with Matt and Cormac. They'd spoken at length virtually and he'd explained everything, but he needed to see them. Needed to repair at least one of his relationships. He tried to talk business but ended up spilling all the details in a rush.

Any vestige of professionalism was shed like a snake's skin.

They sat in Cormac's office, eating pastries, as he recounted returning to the office after being interviewed by the SFO to pick up some files locked in his desk. How the desk drawers had been forced and looted.

He'd strode into Christopher's office and handed in his resignation.

Christopher had laughed in his face. Then his features had hardened.

"If I were a violent man, I'd break your legs," he'd said coldly. "Lucky for you, I'm not. But I'll enjoy ruining you."

Jake had left before security had the chance to throw him out.

They talked about how Evie wanted him to leave her alone.

By the time the office day was done, he was wrung out. Emotionally drained. He'd headed out to his car, intent on booking back into the hotel and spending a depressing week alone.

But Cormac had other ideas.

Which is how he came to be lying once again on Cormac's sofa, wondering how life had come to this.

At the sound of the key in the lock, he switched from horizontal to vertical and turned off the rerun of *Bonanza*. Cormac walked in, Matt close behind.

"No more of this, boyo." Matt walked planted his hands on his hips. "You've wallowed for two days. Will you give up so easily?"

They kicked him into the shower. Made him change his clothes. Then all three sat down at the kitchen table.

"Do you want her?" Cormac asked.

"I want her more than I've ever wanted anything in my entire life. But she doesn't trust me. She won't talk to me." Sadness flooded him. "I don't know how to change her mind."

"You don't need to change her mind. You just have to let her see that you're not a bad guy. You're someone who had to hide the truth so those guys at Global would be stopped."

Jake walked to the window and cracked it open a fraction. "That's another thing. It could be all for nothing. I had a call from one of the detectives investigating the case. They still don't have enough to bring a prosecution."

The very real possibility existed that Global Innovations would walk away unscathed. Jake may have flushed his career and any possibility of finding employment elsewhere without Global suffering any consequences of their corruption. He might have lost Evie for nothing. Another wave of sadness flooded over him.

"They must have screwed up somewhere. It's just a case of finding out where." Cormac was encouraging.

"I can't believe you moved out of the house." Matt frowned. "I'm sure Evie loves you. I could tell just by the way she looks at you."

"She does. She's said so."

"Well then." Matt planted his hands on his hips. "What are you doing about it?"

Jake had spent the hours since the phone calls lying on the sofa missing Evie and wishing he lived in a fantasy black and white world with Little Joe and Hoss. Matt might be the eternal romantic, but he was right. If Jake wanted to change the situation and win her back, he would have to risk everything and put it all on the line.

"I need your help."

Matt clapped Cormac on the back. Both brothers grinned. "That's the spirit. What's next?"

Chapter Twenty-Four

The night before Eleanore was due back, Evie received a voice mail message.

"I'll be back tomorrow morning around ten. I've been in contact with Eleanore and she and Felix will be back in the afternoon. I'm making dinner at seven. I hope you can make it."

She listened to the message four times.

The following day she had the morning from hell. The Duck broke down halfway down one of Dublin's busiest streets. The passengers started off roaring at passing pedestrians, and ended up roaring at her and Oscar when the tour had to be abandoned.

It was a complete nightmare.

She'd missed lunch. Then she got caught in an unexpected downpour and her packed-full bus had sailed past her at the bus stop. She was so wet. There was no point in buying an umbrella and sheltering beneath it. The next bus wasn't due for twenty-five minutes, by which time she could be home if she started walking now.

Rain dripped on the top of her head, travelled through her hair to run in little rivulets down her face. Her shoes made squishy sounds as she walked. An overenthusiastic driver rushing to beat the lights hit a puddle straight on and drowned her in a majestic spray of rainwater.

She was beyond caring.

Instead, she wondered about Jake's message.

Jake had never cooked dinner for them before. Yes, he'd taken her and Eleanore out to dinner in a couple of fancy restaurants. And he'd brought home expensive takeaway, and assembled sausages, bacon, and fried egg into what he called 'a breakfast fit for a king'.

But prepared a meal for all of them? This was new.

Her key was in the lock when the door swung open. Evie stumbled forwards, colliding with Jake's hard torso.

"I saw you coming." He wrapped a large, fluffy bath towel around her. "Grab a shower and I'll make you a coffee."

"Okay." She kicked off her shoes and left them next to the door.

When she came out of the shower fifteen minutes later, it was to find a cup of steaming coffee on her bedside table. She drank it as she dried her hair and dressed.

Music wafted up the staircase. She followed it into the sitting room. Eleanore and Felix sat on the armchairs clutching glasses of what looked like sherry. She fixed herself one from the tray in the corner and joined their conversation.

"This is exciting." Eleanore's eyes twinkled.

"It might well be inedible." Jake had missed so many chances to socialise with Felix, the older man was wary.

"Everyone has to start somewhere," Eleanore said. "You were no great shakes when you started."

Felix drained his sherry. "I suppose true enough. There were some disasters in the early days."

"And we all ate them, anyway. Because that's what friends do. Remember when you made macaroni cheese for me and Rita and she broke a tooth? That was some meal."

"I'm sure Evie doesn't want to hear about that." Felix pivoted. "You got soaked on the way home, did you?"

She briefly recapped the day then Felix and Eleanore shared about their week away.

Jake stuck his head around the door. "Dinner's ready."

A feast adorned the table. Pakora, naans, chapati. A tower of pappadoms and miniature bowls of raita. Basmati. And three dishes which Evie couldn't identify. It all smelled divine. Disappointment shouldn't be on the menu, but she couldn't help but feel it. He'd said he was cooking not—

"Did you make this?" Eleanore pulled back a chair.

"With the help of my friends, yes." They all sat, and he explained each dish and helped everyone load their plates. "I decided to invest in a new restaurant with Matt and Cormac."

"Veda's?" Evie loaded her plate with more rice.

"Yes. She found a premises, and wanted to celebrate." He smiled. "Matt asked her to run a private cookery class as thanks."

"For you?" Felix asked.

"For all three of us. Matt's proficient in the kitchen but with a limited repertoire. I eat out all the time, and Cormac seems to live on beans on toast. We decided it was time to up our game." He slanted her a look and a quick wink.

Maybe she imagined the wink.

Surely she imagined it.

"Well, it's delicious." Eleanore was evidently enjoying every mouthful. "Good man."

"You even made all this?" Evie waved at the sides.

"Yes. I cooked the mains right now, but made the side dishes this afternoon. We made a ton of them. Cormac is eating like a king tonight. And Lisa won't know what's hit her."

He offered chilled water from a carafe in the centre of the table. "I wanted to talk to you all about my work stuff."

"You've told us about it." Eleanore brushed it off. "I don't think we need to know any more."

"I'd like to hear more." Felix dabbed the side of his mouth with his napkin. "Your grandmother's told me a little about what's gone on, but I'd like to hear it from the horse's mouth."

"The company I work for, Global Innovations, mislead me. They signed companies knowing they would decimate the workforce, and they didn't give a damn about being held accountable. I persuaded companies to sign who were later purged for their tech and broken up."

"You didn't mean to, though." The words burst from Evie, unbidden. He couldn't take the blame for something he didn't know was happening. He might be a liar, but he had lied for a reason.

"You weren't aware?" Felix fixed him with a stare.

"No. I was unaware. I thought when they promised to uphold the company's values, they would do so." His lips curled, reliving, and regretting the past.

"What have you done about this?" Felix folded his napkin and placed it next to his plate.

"It's complicated."

Eleanore leant forward and spoke in a quiet voice. "Felix was a high court judge, dear. He might have some good advice."

After dinner, Felix and Jake took over the sitting room and became engrossed in conversation. Jake rolled up the crossword mat, pulled out a sheaf of papers, and laid them out on the table.

Felix asked for a notebook and took notes.

Jake didn't try to minimise or sugar coat anything. His voice was businesslike and dispassionate as he recounted events. He explained about gathering confidential information with the help of his secretary. How he had travelled to the American Head Office and how he and his lawyer had felt intimated when they left.

He talked of his return to his office in London and how his

desk had been broken into and files removed. When he recounted what Christopher had told him before he left, Evie's blood ran cold.

As though reading her mood, Jake turned to her. "I never meant to lie to you. There was too much at stake."

"A lot of this is very questionable morally, but not illegal." Felix picked up a page and examined it in more detail. "And because no contract was ever signed with Sweeney Brothers, they haven't broken any laws."

"What about companies that they have signed contracts with?" Energy was sparking off Jake as he considered new possibilities. "What if we can find proof of their duplicity that resulted in job losses like Barden Ltd. Or even worse, catastrophic company liquidation? Cormac was wary of Global at the beginning. We talked yesterday, and he said it was because he was warned to be cautious by the boss of Barden."

Felix made a note. "You need to dig deep. Retrieve whatever documentation you can, by whatever means you can. Legal, of course. And track down these rumours and interview the other companies who passed on the opportunity to take up Global's offer. You'll need a private investigator to help."

"I can help too." Evie didn't know what she could do, but she wanted to try.

"What's the status of contract negotiations between Global and Sweeney Brothers?" Felix flicked through the papers.

"I—I don't—"

"Global don't know that you've kept them in the loop about everything, do they?" Felix pinned Jake with an intent stare.

"No. They don't." Jake ran a hand through his hair. "They've spent a lot of time and money trying to take over Sweeney Brothers. It figures that they'll try to blacken my name and shift another player in to close the deal."

"There's a lot to do." Felix scrawled on the paper. "Eleanore, tomorrow morning I need to you call Rita and get the contact details for that grandson of hers who's a private investigator. Call me with it."

He switched his attention to Evie. "Evie, it's not beyond the bounds of possibility that Global are monitoring Jake's movements. He can't be seen visiting the Sweeney Brothers' offices. So tomorrow I want you to go and talk to the brothers and inform them of the situation. They should expect an approach."

"I could call them—"

Felix shook his head. "Your calls could be being monitored."

"You can't mean that." Jake's brow pleated.

"We'll soon find out. I'll contact the PI and organise a meet here. The first thing he'll do is screen your electronics, and we'll go from there." He closed the notebook. Steepled his fingers. "These contracts are big money. There's a lot to win and a lot to lose. Don't underestimate the danger here. I'm exhausted. I need to go home."

Everyone stood.

"Thanks for everything, Felix." Jake forced a shaky smile. "You don't know how much this means to me."

Eleanore accompanied Felix to the front door.

Evie turned to Jake. "You don't have to go through with this. You could just walk away." The thought of Jake coming to harm was too much to bear. "You're out now and Matt and Cormac's business is safe."

"But what about the next company they decide to acquire?" Jake took a step closer. He gazed into her eyes. "I have to bring them down." He brushed his thumb over the curve of her jaw. The urge to lean in to his touch, to surrender to the attraction burning bright within, was almost impossible to resist. Evie's eyes closed.

Jake's hand fell from her face. He took a step back. "We need to concentrate all our energies on bringing them down. If what Felix suspects is true, we need to be on our guard. The first matter of business for the private investigator is to make sure they aren't monitoring my devices and have discounted me as a threat. To keep you all safe, I should probably move back to the hotel."

Evie opened her mouth to speak, but he spoke first.

"But I won't. I'm done with hiding. I'm done with any and all barriers between us. I promised I'd never lie to you again, and I meant it. I won't lie. Not even by omission. We're all in this together. I'm not going anywhere."

Chapter Twenty-Five

"Thank you all for coming."

Jake had rented a conference room in Canary Wharf and invited the owners of eight companies who had tangled with Global Innovations. He led a team. Matt and Cormac sat on his right. Suzette, Felix, and Jake's investigator on the left. In his role as financial analyst, Jake had been in each of these companies. Back then, he'd been all business, focused on the numbers rather than the people. He'd overseen signings. Where once he'd been proud of his business success, he now felt shame at being complicit in these companies' troubles. However unwittingly.

Nerves clenched in his stomach. "I've met you all separately for discussions about this situation."

The faces around the table indicated agreement.

"First of all, I want to tell you how sorry I am that I misrepresented Global's intentions."

He braced for censure. But the room stayed silent.

"Some of you signed—"

Josiah Barden, head of Barden Enterprises, the company whose workforce had been reduced by half, raised his hand. "We're big boys and girls here, Jake."

A ripple of agreement travelled around the room.

"Yes, you gave us the impression that Global would act honourably, but you're just one man. One piece of the puzzle. It was on all of us to do our due diligence. Some did, some didn't. that's on us." He looked around the room. "We're not here for apologies. We're here for justice."

"Good. Justice is our aim too." Jake indicated the team on his left. "You've all met my legal team." He held up a copy of a report. Each attendee had an identical report in front of them. "The devil is in the details. We haven't found it yet, but it's there."

It must be. He had to save other companies from damage by Global's predatory practices.

"If you'd like to all turn to page one, I'll run through the documentation we'll need from you all. Our team is standing by to check through all emails and reports you received from Global looking for proof. It might be something small, something easily overlooked. But be reassured, we'll find it."

Jake glanced to his right. Matt smiled. Cormac muttered, "Well said. Good man."

Ten days later, Evie and Soo were putting on make-up in Soo's bathroom. The apartment she and Alex had moved into wasn't large, but had the most impressive bathroom either of them had ever seen.

Twin porcelain sinks adorned one wall. Above them, a wide mirror surrounded by light bulbs spanned both sinks. The wall opposite was similarly mirrored.

"I feel like I'm in that movie *Moulin Rouge*." Evie checked her sky-blue eyeshadow then carefully stuck on fake lashes.

The bathroom was so huge, there was even space for chairs before the mirror. Soo perched on one. "What's the latest?"

"It's crazy at home. Eleanore insisted that Jake take over her late husband's office on the top floor and it has become command central. He has debriefings ever day with a private investigator. Matt and Cormac arrive every evening and stay for hours. They all flew to London last week for meetings."

"Sounds intense." She shot a glance in Evie's direction in the mirror. "You and he haven't..."

"Not so much as a kiss." Evie sighed. "I guess I told him to stay out of my way."

"You did." Soo fiddled with her hair.

"But that was when I was angry with him for lying. I now have a better idea of why he did what he did." Something twisted in her stomach at the memory of him being threatened. "I don't want to lose him."

"Did you tell him?"

"I didn't get the chance. He says we should stay away from each until this thing is over." Evie dabbed on shiny lipgloss. "I've learnt from the past. When that moment comes, I won't hold back. I want us to be together, and I think he wants that, too."

"Aren't you sure?"

"All he seems to want at the moment is to destroy his old company."

So much was uncertain. They both had a tendency to run, rather than to talk things through. But he had been true to his word, and kept the lines of communication open even when the news was worrying.

"Eleanore asked me what I'd think of her offering another home share agreement."

"To Jake?" Soo's eyebrows rose.

There was a rap on the bathroom door. "Are you girls ready yet?"

Evie zipped up her white leather boots. Soo opened the door. Alex stood in the doorway, hands on hips.

"Do I look ridiculous in this?" He walked in and faced the mirror.

"You look perfect." Soo stroked the white satin over his shoulders.

"It feels weird." He readjusted himself. "I feel sort of exposed."

"Tell me about it. Remind me not to bend over." Evie cast a critical eye over her short white satin tunic with a large blue cat emblazoned on the front.

Soo stood on the other side of Alex and snapped a picture of them all on her cell phone. "I can't wait to see the Alphas in platforms."

Chapter Twenty-Six

"We're never going to get them, are we?" A deep sense of depression settled in Jake's chest. The team had managed to process much more information than he would have been able to on his own, but all for naught. Global was going to escape without any consequences, and there was nothing he could do about it.

Cormac pushed back his chair and grabbed three beers from the fridge.

"Never say never." He took his Swiss Army knife out of his pocket and found the right tool. Then he flipped the cap off the bottles and handed them around.

"Just leave it on the desk." Matt was hunched over, staring at a monitor. "There's something weird about this spreadsheet."

Interest sparked. Jake scooted his swivel chair to Matt's desk. "What are you looking at?"

"The future projections that Global sent to Edjicore." He pointed at the screen. "The column references—"

"Hidden columns." Jake took over. Global often put their information in columns on a spreadsheet but hid the ones they didn't need to see. It was normal practice to make sure to remove columns with sensitive information before sending files to clients.

Jake made the columns visible. "This is it." The hidden columns showed exactly how much increased profitability would be gained by culling the workforce. One column for ten per cent, one for twenty, and one for thirty.

"It was attached to this email." Matt pointed the way. They all read it silently on the screen.

"They talk about increasing profits without sacking staff. But the spreadsheet shows they were factoring in job losses of thirty per cent." Jake looked from one to the other. "I've got that right, haven't I?" He felt lightheaded. As though he was short of air.

"Yes." Matt patted him on the back. "Yes. We've done it."

Jake felt like a climber hanging on to a cliff face by his fingernails. He wanted this to be over. Wanted to believe Matt's words and give in to an overwhelming sense of relief. But he needed to be sure.

"Felix and Eleanore are watching TV downstairs. Could you ask him to come up?"

With an affirmative grunt, Cormac headed for the door.

Jake called Suzette. It was early on a Friday evening. A time when someone might well expect their lawyer wouldn't be available. "I'll be straight over."

Matt stared at the screen. "It was a pure fluke I noticed."

Whoever had sent that email and attached the spreadsheet must have only the most rudimentary understanding of the program. Jake checked to see who exactly had forwarded the information. Christopher. That tracked.

"If he left hidden cells in a spreadsheet once, he could have done it again. We'll have to go through all the email attachments again."

"Tomorrow. We'll start tomorrow." Jake reached for the beer left forgotten on the table. "Tonight, it's enough to just show this to Felix and Suzette. More can wait."

Within half an hour, he'd received the confirmation he needed. Suzette would run a team checking all the attachments and liaise with the SFO and the London police. Felix felt confident that the case against Global was solid.

Everything was at last right with the world. Except one thing.

Jake turned to Eleanore. "Where's Evie?"

"Out with her friend Soo. She said they were going to that nightclub she went to for her birthday."

"Crap." He didn't know it. He'd missed her bloody birthday, chasing this case.

"Blaze," Matt said. "The club is called Blaze." He smiled. "Cormac and I went to her party. Remember?"

"Do you want to come?"

Matt shook his head. "You better change, though. They've got a strict dress code."

Cormac declined, too. "All I want is my bed, mate."

Jake needed to pass the head of the queue on the way to the end of the line. The moment he walked up, he knew he was in trouble. But he asked the bouncer, anyway. "Will I get in?" He pointed at himself. He'd taken Matt's advice and smartened up. Had worn dress shoes rather than sneakers. It wouldn't be enough.

The bouncer's smile stretched wide. He shook his head slowly. "No way."

Evie was in there. Somewhere. He had to get in.

Jake joined the end of the line. A group of three in front of him turned to look.

"You won't get in," a woman said.

"I didn't know." An idea sparked. "Hey." He looked at the man in their midst. He was about the same height as Jake, skinnier, but it could work. "Can I buy your clothes? You can have mine."

"I wouldn't get in then."

"Maybe just half of your outfit. I'll give you a hundred euro for those trousers." Never in his life did he imagine he'd be offering a hundred euro for a pair of skin-tight red satin trousers.

"I made those." The other girl looked offended.

"I wouldn't think of selling them." Her boyfriend flung an arm around her shoulders. "No sale."

"Anything else? Could anyone sell me anything that would get me dressed up enough to get in?"

They shook their heads, so Jake took his request to the masses. He stepped out of the line and pulled cash from his pocket. "Would anyone sell me their clothes?" He waved the cash in the air, like a lottery winner. "You can have mine."

Half the queue ignored him. The other half talked quietly, no doubt evaluating if he was drunk, mad. or both. The queue shuffled forwards and No one responded.

"Please." He reached out to a guy wearing platform heels and flares inset with shimmering sequin inserts. "Could I just borrow your jacket?"

"Get your hands off me." The guy shoved, fast and hard, propelling Jake onto his ass in the gutter. Everyone ignored him and kept walking.

Where could he get something to wear at this hour? Jake stood. He hung his head, deep in thought.

"What's your problem, baby?" A group of four drag artists wandered over. They all looked spectacular.

"I need to get in there. Can I buy some part of one of your costumes—I—"

"This isn't a costume, it's a whole look."

"It's fantastic. You look brilliant."

"You should have put in more effort." The redhead looked him up and down. "You haven't tried at all."

"I didn't know! I had no idea, okay? I have to get in there." Desperation clawed at his gut. He couldn't walk away and let another night go by without telling Evie how much he loved her. "For all I know she's in there dancing with another guy."

"There's a girl?" The blonde flicked back a swathe of poker straight hair and leant in.

"Not just a girl, the girl. The only girl in the world for me. I need to get in there and tell her I love her. I just hope it's not too late."

"How did you get here? Do you have a car?"

"It's around the corner." Maybe they were going to take him somewhere. Back to someone's house where a treasure trove of sparkly clothes filled a wardrobe.

"Take us there."

"This way." He'd parked illegally on the street, willing to get a ticket or clamped if it meant he could get in to see Evie as soon as possible.

The troupe sauntered along behind him. All four towered over him in their platform boots. A man walking along the opposite side of the street was so distracted by the sight he walked into a lamppost.

"This is me." He stopped at the car.

"Open up, babe. And strip."

It seemed wrong to be getting naked with people when he didn't even know their names. "I'm Jake."

He chucked his clothes into the back seat. Stripped off his socks and shoes. Stood in the middle of the pavement in black briefs and nothing else. The four looked at him, then at their own outfits as though he were a dress up doll.

"I'm Peter, but you can call me Björn."

"We're in character tonight." The blonde pointed at herself. "Agnetha. Or Anna, whichever you prefer. Benny, and Frida. Got it?"

"Got it."

"We can't do anything about his feet. And those shoes are brutal."

"I have a pair of Vans in my sports bag in the back." He opened the boot and retrieved them. They were plain black.

"Hand 'em over." Agnetha opened her handbag and pulled out a tube of glittery either lipstick or eye shadow. He had no idea which. "I'll bedazzle them."

Benny gave him a frank appraisal. "Without a wig, he can't do either of the girls."

"We don't have to be literal, right? I mean, Björn would rock this short tunic and bare legs, wouldn't he?" Björn shimmied out of his flares and handed them to Jake.

Jake checked out Björn's legs. "You look fantastic."

Björn grinned. "Hold onto your hat, you will too."

The jeans fit okay length wise but were so tight Jake would be well capable of singing soprano. He rearranged his package for the umpteenth time.

Agnetha slapped his hand away. "Stop playing with yourself. It's distracting." She swept a line of glitter across his chest and blended it in.

Benny was doing something to Jake's hair with gel. "You don't have to be a member of the band, you just have to be going with the whole aesthetic." He stepped back to admire his handiwork. "Oh, that's much better." He looked down at his own outfit. "I guess I could lend you my waistcoat." He looked disappointed.

"He looks better bare," Frida said.

"Gimme your phone." Björn held out a hand.

Jake complied.

"Here's my number and my address. Send me back my flares, okay?"

"Yes."

Agnetha reached for his hand. "Come on, let's do this!"

Chapter Twenty-Seven

ive me a man after midnight.

Evie checked her watch. Five past, and here he was. Striding her direction with a glint in his blue eyes and a smile that would seduce even the coldest heart. He wore an electric-blue pleather suit with a bare chest beneath and fabulous gold platforms.

"Heyyy." Wyatt snaked an arm around her waist and pulled her close. "You look bangin'." He nuzzled into her neck and pressed a kiss there.

Evie's body responded to the familiar touch of him, the feel of his body against hers. Her mind and her heart however, didn't.

She placed her palm flat against his naked chest and flexed her fingers. Gave a tiny push. Not big enough to be noticed by anyone but him.

Wyatt looked up. Close up she could scent the alcohol on his breath. See the glaze in his eyes a second before he closed them with a grimace. "Oh shit, I'm being inappropriate, aren't I?"

"Just a tiny bit." Part of her still loved him. How could it not?

Wyatt took a step away.

"You look great." Evie removed her hand from him and readjusted the white tie-belt at her waist to give her hands something to do.

"I've been looking for you all night." Wyatt's words were a little slurred as he shouted over the music. "Damien said you were wearing a blonde wig, but half the people here are, so it's been impossible."

"Is your girlfriend here?"

His mouth turned down at the corners. "Didn't work out."

The music changed. Wyatt grabbed her hand. "Oh, come on, I love this one!"

Soo and the Alphas had the same idea. They lined up in a row, alongside the other revellers on the dance floor.

"This one's easy. Start with your left."

'Lay All Your Love on Me' blared from the speakers.

"Side side front back switch,' Evie muttered, watching the person in the line in front of her. "Jump jump side side front back shit."

"Keep going!" Soo yelled. It was alright for her. She was blessed with perfect rhythm and her feet just seemed to know what to do. Evie cast her gaze sideways. The Alphas moved as one, as if they were part of a flash mob.

Wyatt grabbed her hand again. "Side side front back!"

Even bloody Wyatt nailed it.

The temptation to stop dancing and just do an ABBA sway was strong. But Evie resisted. She could do it. The song wasn't very long, she just had to concentrate.

Side side. Damn, wrong side wrong side. She crashed into Damien and her misstep travelled all the way up the entire line of dancers, causing a murmur of discontent.

"Found you."

She looked up to see Jake facing her.

"Come on." He reached his hands out and she grabbed them

and escaped the line. The song was ending, but the opening bars of 'Dancing Queen' had everyone stomping already.

She gripped Jake's hand as he strode through the crowds and pushed open an emergency door to the outside.

Only then did she have the chance to *really* look at him. His hair was swept back in a windswept style. His bare chest was covered in some sort of shiny glitter and his stomach rippled with muscles. Worn denim flares hugged his narrow hips and clung to his thighs. Lines of rhinestone studs travelled down the outside of both thighs. Sequinned inserts started just at his knees and he seemed to be wearing sparkly runners, too.

Evie licked her dry lips. She hadn't thought she had a thing for glam rockers, but the look of Jake was fast changing her mind.

Jake's hand was on her chin. "Look up here."

She tilted her face up to his.

The look in his eyes stole her breath. It was love, want, mine, all at once. "I found you. I didn't even know you were Agnetha tonight." He stroked her lip. "I've accosted half the women here and a couple of guys. I came to find you. It couldn't wait until tomorrow. I couldn't wait another moment to tell you that the whole Global fiasco is over. We've got them. Now all I need is you."

He took a deep breath. Something caught his attention back in the club through the glass door and he smiled.

Evie followed his gaze. A group of four excellent ABBA clones stood staring at them. Jake waved, and they delivered thumbs ups.

Jake turned back to give Evie his full attention. "I love you. I want to live with you." His mouth curved in a smile that kicked her heartbeat up a notch. "Unfortunately, that also means living with my grandmother and your cat. So I guess what I really mean is, will you home share with me?"

"Home wouldn't be home without you in it. Kiss me." She puckered up and went up on tiptoe.

Jake's hands clasped her satin clad bottom and pulled her close.

Behind his head, she could see the moon and the stars sparkling. Then his lips found hers, her eyes closed, and nothing else in the whole damn world mattered.

Six months later – December

We have seven days.

In seven days, we'll be hosting Christmas.

Jake stood behind the royal blue velvet curtain and peeked out at the audience. He couldn't see anyone he knew, but their friends were there. All of them.

Years ago, the house of Bedford Street on Christmas Day had been the hub for many. Eleanore and her husband had opened their doors to their friends and also to those alone or lonely. Everyone had contributed something to the Christmas get together. Strangers brought by friends had woven their own threads into the rich tapestry of Eleanore's life.

The year before last, Eleanore, Rita and Felix had celebrated with crispy duck from M&S.

Last year, they'd roasted a chicken and sat around the kitchen table wearing paper hats.

This year, Evie and Jake had volunteered to help. The guest list was bulging at the seams. As was the ever-expanding list of things to be done to be ready to greet friends and family.

Home Share. They shared a home. And for one day, would

share that home with friends who had become family. And strangers who might.

Music started. A man walked onto the stage and stood looking out into the audience with his arms open wide. Thin streaks of white were just visible in his sandy hair and his beard. He wore a red shirt tucked into faded jeans with a brightly coloured woven fabric belt tied around his waist.

A wave of love and joy flowed from the audience to him. Finn's Christmas concert was a tradition in the city. A deep and true connection flowing from year to year. Some of the players drifted away, some took up instruments and joined him on the stage. In a world full of change, the constancy of his concert planted seeds of hope in people's hearts that the good things in life might survive another year.

"Hello!"

The answering 'hello' shouted back made Jake smile. Finn held the audience in the palm of his hand. "We'll start playing in a few minutes, but before that, I want to introduce someone special." He looked to the opposite side of the stage. "For many years, the incomparable Maggie Andrews would join me on stage every Christmas and play her beautiful harp for us all. We lost Maggie two years ago, but this year, I've persuaded her daughter, Evie, to play something on her mother's harp for us." He held up his hands to stop the crowd from responding until he was finished. "Evie hasn't played on stage before. She's nervous. Let's show her there's nothing to be afraid of."

The audience clapped.

Evie walked out onto the stage and embraced Finn, and the audience applause swelled, filling the space.

Finn left the stage. Evie settled behind the harp and rested her fingers on the strings.

All sound fell away to be replaced by a silence so deep and absolute it was as though everyone was holding their breath.

Evie glanced over to the place Jake stood. Even at a distance, he could see the tension in her shoulders release a fraction. A faint smile played across her lips.

She'd asked him to be there. To be where she could see him and draw strength from his presence. Just as her mother had asked Evie to stand in the shadows, behind the curtain at the side of the stage at her concerts.

"I need to see a little piece of my heart as I play," Evie'd said.

Jake had seen videos of her mother playing everything from traditional Irish music to classics on the harp. Evie hadn't wanted to learn anything like that, so she'd learned her favourite songs translated for the harp by her talented mother.

This was her favourite.

'Careless Whisper's' melodic harmonies drifted from the harp's strings.

The moment after she'd agreed to play at the concert, panic had set in. Evie had known the notes, but long abstinence from playing had stiffened her fingers and made her playing hesitant.

Fear of performing in public had been crippling, too.

She'd worked hard, practicing every evening. She played every week while the Knit Nuts knitted, the clack of needles providing an interesting accompaniment to Evie's music.

And tonight, she was perfect.

The final notes fell from her fingertips. A moment of silence hung in the air.

Then the audience leapt to their feet, and thunderous applause rang out.

Her gaze searched out and met his. He mouthed *I love you*, and she mouthed it back.

Finn thanked the crowd and Evie and hugged her tight. Musicians and stagehands scurried around, preparing for the next part of the concert.

Jake's fingers closed around the little navy box in his pocket. If big, flashy proposals in front of crowds of strangers was his thing, now would be the perfect time. He could step up on stage, get down on one knee, and ask Evie to marry him in front of all these people.

She'd be embarrassed.

They'd talked about kids and growing old together. He had no doubts about what her answer would be.

They had seven days.

In the home they shared, in front of all the people who mattered, he'd ask her.

And she'd say yes.

THE END